Nolan's Law

After his mother and father die, and the girl he hopes to marry turns him down, Jude James decides to abandon his rented homestead and ride for the West. Before he can leave, though, Josh Appleseed – a young ex-slave – arrives on a stolen horse seeking sanctuary. They ride West together.

The unscrupulous owner of a farm sends his gunslingers in pursuit which leads to a showdown in which one of the gunslingers and a tracker-dog are killed.

As they continue on, Jude and Josh fall in with Brod Nolan and his gang. Nolan claims to rob the rich to feed the poor, but with Nolan there is more than meets the eye, and the two friends find themselves embroiled in a series of blood-curdling encounters in which they must kill or be killed. Will they emerge unscathed?

By the same author

Shoot-out at Big King
Man of Blood
Riders From Hell
Time to Kill
Blood on the Sand
A Town Called Perdition
Incident at River Bend
The Proving of Matt Stowe

Nolan's Law

Lee Lejeune

A Black Horse Western
ROBERT HALE

© Lee Lejeune 2016
First published in Great Britain 2016

ISBN 978-0-7198-1888-2

The Crowood Press
The Stable Block
Crowood Lane
Ramsbury
Marlborough
Wiltshire SN8 2HR

www.crowood.com

Robert Hale is an imprint of
The Crowood Press

The right of Lee Lejeune to be identified as
author of this work has been asserted by him
in accordance with the Copyright, Designs
and Patents Act 1988

Typeset by
Derek Doyle & Associates, Shaw Heath
Printed and bound in Great Britain by
CPI Antony Rowe, Chippenham and Eastbourne

CHAPTER ONE

Jude James was looking west as he had many times before. Somewhere over the horizon lay a land of great undulating plains, beyond which were high impenetrable mountains capped by snow. Jude had soared across those plains and snow-capped mountains many times before in his imagination, but now, suddenly, they seemed to beckon more urgently; he knew he had reached a crossroad in his life and either had to turn back or go on towards those beckoning plains and crags.

Jude was just twenty years old. He had reddish hair that hung down almost to his shoulders, so that some of his friends called him 'Ginger' James and others, more disparagingly 'Carrot Top'. Jude didn't mind the disparagement too much. He reckoned he had quite a lot going for him. He was around six feet tall and as strong as Hercules. He was a good wrestler and had been bright at school, though he hadn't stayed there long enough to find out just how bright he was.

Trouble was, his pa had died three years back after being trampled by a big farm horse and his ma had teamed up again with a big bruiser of a man who cared for his drink a little too much, especially the hooch whiskey he got from a neighbour who ran a still in his barn. That hooch whiskey was lethal and it had been known to blind a man who drank too much of it. One of the neighbours had stumbled out into the dark on one freezing night after a skinfull and disappeared completely. They had found him stiff as a chopping board in a ditch a couple of days later. Old Hennessey, who ran the still, was hauled out protesting and given a thorough beating by the farmer's brother a week later but that didn't stop the hooch drinking. Ed Shadwell, Jude's mother's new partner, continued, falling into a drunken stupor for days on end. He was no use to any man or woman, or beast, for that matter.

Jude knew in teaming up with Shadwell his ma had made the biggest mistake of her life and he stayed on at the farm hoping that bum Shadwell would eventually be kicked right out.

Then three events occurred to make Jude change his mind. The first was that his ma took to drinking the moonshine with Ed Shadwell, which meant she was often out cold for days on end as well, so that Jude had to do most of the work around the farm on his own. That wouldn't have mattered since Jude was good and more than capable, except that they didn't own the farm. It was on lease from a carpetbagger from the north who had got rich from buying up land after the recent war. Jude had never met Mcdee, the carpetbagger, but he knew his agent, a certain Ben Maddock who showed up regularly, accompanied by two sinister-looking *hombres* to collect the rent.

In fact, while Jude was looking west towards the distant plains that day, Ben Maddock showed up with his two sidekicks. The three rode right up to the cabin and Maddock looked over it just like he owned it.

'Good morrow,' he said, superciliously.

'Good morning, Mr Maddock,' Jude replied, politely.

'Where's your folk?' Maddock demanded, in a superior tone.

Jude looked over the two hard-faced *hombres* and they stared right back at him through half closed eyes. 'My ma's inside,' he said. 'Resting up.'

'Resting up,' Maddock said contemptuously. 'You mean she's been sipping at that moonshine again with that there new pa of yours.'

Jude felt the hackles on the back of his neck rising. 'I said she's resting up,' he said defiantly. 'I don't think I mentioned anything more.'

Maddock looked down at him and sneered. 'You got a lot of lip on you, Ginger Boy. How old are you?'

Jude paused for a moment and then said 'I'm about as old as my toes and a little older than my front teeth.'

'Is that so?' Maddock said. He turned to his two sidekicks. 'You hear that, boys? We got a real wise guy here.'

The two sidekicks were still looking at Jude without the flicker of a smile. He knew they were armed and would be happy to use their guns if needs be. He also knew that he could lick them clean if they got off their horses, but such thoughts were foolish and had to be pushed to one side.

'So what can I do for you, Mr Maddock?' he asked again.

'What you can do for me, Ginger Top, is hand over the rent you owe me,' Maddock said. 'Soon as you done that, me and the boys can ride out of here and leave you to get on with the common round.'

Jude looked up and grinned. 'I'm afraid I'll have to trouble you to come back next month when my ma's feeling a little better because right now we don't have the money available.'

Maddock looked at his two sidekicks again and considered the matter. 'Well, Ginger Top, Mr Mcdee ain't gonna like that one little bit. Right now you owe two months' rent with interest. Things are mounting up and you know what happens when a tenant gets out of his depth, don't you? There are plenty of others lined up to take his place.'

Jude stiffened. 'I guess I can figure things out as well as the next man,' he said.

'Sure you can,' Maddock agreed ironically. He turned his horse and looked back over his shoulder. 'Give your ma my regards,' he said. 'Tell her to keep off that poisonous comfort juice and make sure you got the money next month when we come on by.'

The two sidekicks nodded with grim innuendo and the three men rode slowly away.

The second thing that happened was that Jude rode into town for the local shindig. Jude had an excellent sense of rhythm and he liked to dance. In fact, he had quite a good reputation among the ladies, and one young lady in particular. She was Lucy Hendry the doctor's daughter. Jude knew only too well that Lucy was too good for him. She was from a different class altogether, but there was definitely a mutual attraction between them. Lucy was a fine-looking girl with dark hair and a flashing smile. Doctor and Mrs Hendry had sent her to the very best school in the state.

As soon as Jude saw her he knew that he wanted her above all things, but he also knew that what he had hoped for was well out of his reach. Nevertheless, he bowed graciously and asked her to dance.

'I'd love to,' she said in the low voice that made his heart skip a beat. And away they went, in and out and round about with the other dancers. Each time they drew close Lucy smiled enticingly and drew away again. When Jude escorted her to her seat, her father and mother scrutinized him closely. Doctor Hendry smiled at him politely but without particular warmth.

Although Jude knew that Lucy was beyond his grasp he

had dreamed that they might run away together and someday he would make a pile of money and keep them, if not in luxury at least in reasonable comfort. Now his dreams were to be shattered like fine glass when Lucy said, 'Mr James, I want you to meet somebody.' She turned to a young man who was sleek and probably the most smartly dressed man in room. He was as tall as Jude and very well presented. Jude thought he looked like an English duke.

'This is Dr Roach, my fiancé, Mr James.'

Jude felt the blood drain from his face, but he bowed politely. 'I'm pleased to meet you, Dr Roach.'

The musicians struck up again and the dancers whirled away like bright lilies floating on the surface of a lake, but Jude didn't join in. He felt sick to his stomach and light in the head. The words *my fiancé* echoed through his brain like the bells tolling at a funeral. So he slipped out of the hall and rode back to the farm where his mother and stepfather were drinking moonshine and playing cards.

Ed Shadwell looked up at him and grinned. 'You're back early, boy,' he said. 'Did something happen to cool your jingle bob?'

Jude looked at his stepfather and knew he despised him. Picturing Lucy Hendry dancing with Roach didn't help much. 'What's my jingle bob to you?' he asked a little more aggressively than he had intended.

Ed Shadwell had already imbibed more of that hooch than was good for him. So he pushed himself up from his chair and thrust out his chin. 'Are you talking to me, boy?' he slurred.

Jude tried to keep himself calm. He could see his ma's expression of appeal as she looked first at Shadwell and then at him. 'Well, I'm certainly not talking to my ma and I'm not talking to myself,' he said. 'And there's only one other person in the room, I believe.'

Shadwell shook his head and gasped in fury. 'You gonna apologize to me, boy, before I teach you a lesson in good manners?'

Jude was aware of his mother looking at him as if to say, 'Please stop this before it gets completely out of hand', but for him it had already gone too far. 'I don't think I need to apologize to you for anything,' he said to Shadwell.

Shadwell staggered back in amazement. 'Well, that's downright disrespectful!' he shouted. 'I'm gonna teach you to respect your elders, boy!' He drew back a hefty fist and took a swing at Jude. If he hadn't been drunk the fist might have connected. In fact it was pretty well on target anyway, But, as it swung in, Jude parried it with his left arm and threw a jab with his right. His fist struck Shadwell on the left cheek and Shadwell staggered away and went down on his back. Shadwell wasn't a small man and, as he went down, he took the chair with him and it broke in pieces. For a moment Shadwell lay panting with a look of amazement on his face as though he wondered where the thunderbolt had come from. Then he coughed and blood started gushing from his nose.

He started to roll over and was struggling to drag himself on to his feet. Jude knew he either had to hit him again or get out of the room. So, in a split second, he backed up and held his fists ready. Though he was a good wrestler he knew he could punch Shadwell into unconsciousness and he was ready for what seemed to be inevitable.

But Shadwell never came rushing in with his hammer-like fists because at that moment Jude's mother cried out in pain and pressed her hand to her side just under her heart.

'Oh God!' she gasped. 'Oh God!' Her face was yellow and her mouth opened with pain and horror as she fell.

*

The two men stared in disbelief as she collapsed behind the table.

Shadwell was the first to speak. 'My God!' he croaked. 'She's had a fit!' He leaned on the table and wiped his arm over his bleeding nose.

Jude didn't bother to reply. He got down on his knees and looked down at his mother and realized she'd had a heart attack. He leaned over her and wondered what he could do to save her.

How do you bring back a person with a heart attack? he asked himself. He pressed his ear to her breast – the breast that had suckled him, and listened. Yes, the heart was beating spasmodically like a bird fluttering against a window pane.

'Keep calm, I will bring you back again,' he told her. Then he pressed his hands against her ribs and started pressing rhythmically.

'What can I do?' he heard Shadwell asking him, as though from a distance.

'What you can do is you can ride into town and ask Doc Hendry to come immediately. He'll know what to do. You think you can do that?' He turned to look at Shadwell and saw that he was in no state to do anything. He was just standing there and shaking and ready to puke. 'Just go out there, get on your horse and ride like hell,' Jude commanded.

Shadwell nodded vaguely but seemed to be nailed to the floor.

'Get out there and ride!' Jude shouted.

Shadwell nodded; then he moved to the door and shambled out.

Dr Hendry was still at the shindig when Shadwell appeared. A man came into the hall and approached the doctor who was taking a refreshment with his wife and daughter and future son-in-law.

'Excuse me, Doctor, there seems to have been an accident There's a man outside wto looks a mess. I think he's been in a fight and he's asking to see you.'

Doctor Henry never refused to see a patient. It was a matter of medical ethics. 'Well, why don't you bring him in?' he said. He looked at his wife and raised his eyebrows as if to say, It's probably nothing but I have to investigate. He went to the door where he saw a rugged individual with a badly swollen and bruised face and his left eye half closed. 'What happened?' he asked. 'Were you hit by a wagon?'

Shadwell didn't even try to smile. His face was too painful. 'She's passed out,' he muttered. 'Had a fit or something.'

'Who passed out?' the doctor asked.

'Mrs James,' Shadwell said. 'Fell down behind the table. Her son Jude is trying to bring her round.'

'Mrs James?' the doctor said. 'Where is she?'

'She's at home lying on the floor. I think she's dying.' Shadwell looked so ghastly he might have been dying himself.

Doctor Hendry didn't ask any further questions. He just grabbed his medical bag and turned to his wife. 'I've got to ride out to the James's place. It seems there's been some kind of accident there.' He hurried out, followed by Shadwell who, despite his size, looked more like a shadow than a Shadwell.

When they reached the farm, Dr Hendry hurried in with his bag and looked for the patient.

'She was over there underneath the table,' Shadwell explained feebly. 'Now she's gone.'

Hendry wondered whether he was the victim of some ill-timed hoax. He noted there was a strong smell of alcohol in the room. Then he heard a voice from the other end of the cabin. 'Through here, Dr Hendry.'

12

The doctor moved to the door and looked into the room where he saw in the light of an oil lamp the figure of a woman lying on a bed. Jude, her son, was standing beside her.

'Thank you for coming, Doctor,' Jude said, 'but I'm afraid you're too late.'

The doctor knelt beside the bed and examined the patient. It was a thorough examination but short. He got up from the bed and looked at Jude with grave concern. 'I'm afraid you're right, Mr James. Your mother has passed away.'

Jude looked down at his mother with reverence but said nothing.

'What happened?' Dr Hendry asked him.

'I think I killed her,' Jude confessed.

Jude knew that he had killed his mother when he launched his fist at Ed Shadwell and it affected him profoundly. Shadwell was a man of straw – a trail bum who had taken advantage of a lonely woman, still pining for her dead husband. But Jude blamed himself: he shouldn't have let that man of straw provoke him. So he made up his mind right away that Shadwell had to leave the farm immediately before they came to blows again, or Shadwell killed him while he was asleep at night. Shadwell seemed to read his mind. So he avoided meeting the younger man's gaze and transferred himself to the barn until after the funeral.

The funeral director, a man called Tut Turtle on account of the fact that he always tutted when he looked at one of his precious bodies, gazed at Jude's ma, and looked really sad. 'Couldn't have happened to a nicer person,' he said. 'So young too!' He looked at Jude with moist eyes. 'How old was she, Mr James?'

'Around forty,' Jude replied. He had no wish to discuss his mother's age or anything else with Tut Turtle, though he appreciated that Turtle was trying to show his professional concern.

'So young!' Turtle sighed. 'Far too young. But we never know when the Good Lord will take us, do we, Mr James?'

'Indeed, we don't,' Jude agreed. In fact he didn't know much about anything at the moment, least of all *the Good Lord.*

The funeral was frugal as it had to be since Jude had very little money. Ed Shadwell proved to be conspicuous by his absence. In fact, a couple of days after Jude's mother's demise he had disappeared completely like any other trail bum.

After Mrs James had been laid in the ground beside her late husband, Dr Hendry came up to Jude and put his hand on his shoulder. 'We live in hard times, Mr James, and your mother had a hard life. What will you do now she's gone?'

Jude pondered for a moment. 'Thank you for your concern, Doctor,' he said. 'To tell you the truth, I have no idea what I will do.'

Doctor Hendry gave him a shrewd, almost fatherly, look. 'You should study, you know. You have a head on your shoulders and a future before you. Don't let it go to waste, my boy.' Doctor Hendry pressed his arm and walked away.

Yes, I have a future, Jude thought, and it's somewhere far away from here and I mean to go and search for it. He thought of his ma and pa lying side by side in that cold grave. What had life given them but toil and hardship? he asked himself.

Next morning he opened the drawer of his father's secret closet and found what he had been looking for – a belt with a Colt revolver in its holster. He drew the gun from the holster and weighed it in his palm. And it fitted just right. It wasn't loaded but there was a box of cartridges at the back of the drawer. So he loaded the single action Colt and strapped on the belt. And again it might have been made for him.

The Colt wasn't an old-fashioned Navy, so it hadn't been used in the recent war. He wondered why his father had had it and what it had been used for. He took it out into the lot and that's when he saw Mcdee's agent Ben Maddock and his two sidekicks riding towards him. They rode right up to the farm but didn't dismount. The two cohorts looked just as grim as before and they said nothing. In fact, Jude had never heard their voices; they might just as well have been two sinister-looking dummies propped up on their horses.

'Good morrow!' Maddock greeted as before, sounding like he had a bad smell at the end of his nose.

'Good morning,' Jude said.

'Heard you beat up on that juice-lover on the property, Carrot Top.'

'We had a slight disagreement,' Jude acknowledged.

Maddock nodded. 'Mr Mcdee asked me to convey his condolences about your mother's unfortunate passing.'

'That's very kind of him,' Jude said. 'Please give him my thanks.'

'I'll do that,' Maddock said with a faint grin. 'I see you're tooled up this morning, Carrot Top.'

'That's right,' Jude replied brightly. 'You never know when you might meet a skunk or a rat, do you, Mr Maddock?'

'That is so,' Maddock said. 'We just wondered what you might do now that your ma's passed on.'

Jude was watching the two sidekicks and he noticed their eyes flickered slightly as they saw the single action Colt on his hip.

'I'm thinking on that, Mr Maddock,' he said.

'And are you thinking about clearing up on that money you owe Mr Mcdee?'

Jude shrugged. 'I haven't thought much on it, Mr Maddock. I have other things on my mind right now.'

'Have you then?' Maddock said, glancing sideways at his men. They stirred as though they were about to dismount. 'I hope you know what happens to folk who don't pay what they owe,' Maddock said.

'I've heard rumours, Mr Maddock, but I don't take much heed of them.'

Maddock nodded and one of the sidekicks made a move to dismount from his horse.

Jude made a sudden decision. He drew the Colt and levelled it and trained it on the man who was about to dismount. It seemed the most natural thing in the world and he amazed himself. 'If I might make a suggestion,' he said, 'I would stay right in the saddle and bide where you are with your hands away from those shooters of yours in case someone gets injured.'

The two seemed to freeze like in a rather dark photograph. Maddock gave a twisted grin. 'My, boy! I do believe you're beginning to grow up. I hope you can use that thing.'

'And I hope I never need to use it, Mr Maddock.'

Maddock turned to his two henchmen. 'OK, boys, there's always another day.' He grinned at Jude. 'Mr Mcdee ain't gonna like this one little bit, you know, Carrot Top.'

Then he gave a high piercing laugh. The two men scowled and the three riders wheeled their horses and rode away.

Jude looked down at the gun in his hand and said, 'I must really learn to use this thing!'

CHAPTER TWO

'As God made little apples, those three gorillas are going to come right back when they think I'm least expecting it,' Jude said to himself. He knew it had happened before. One man had been beaten almost to a pulp when he refused to pay what Mcdee said he owed him. Doc Hendry had patched him up and some said the doc had gone to complain to Mcdee, but it made no difference. 'What keeps me here, anyway?' Jude asked himself. 'Just a few sticks of furniture and a whole heap of memories.'

He went out into the lot and looked west again. That's where the future lies, he thought, somewhere in those rolling hills and plains. It's got to be better than slaving away here. In fact, I might just as well be one of those poor black slaves working in the cotton plantations.

While he was staring wistfully across the blue-hazed hills he saw a faint smudge that turned itself into a rider and the rider was coming straight towards him. Those skookums are coming right back, he thought. But, as he looked, he realized there was only one rider. That didn't mean a thing: the other two might be sneaking up on him from another direction. So he drew the Colt revolver and held it low and crouched down behind a pile of winter logs.

The rider loomed closer and closer until he was so close that Jude might have recognized him. Then he saw that under the broad-brimmed and somewhat dilapidated hat the face was kind of burned umber brown.

Jude cocked the Colt and held it out straight. 'That's far enough!' he warned. 'Don't come any closer. I'm in a somewhat nervous condition and I might just shoot off a round.'

The rider drew rein and said, 'Don't do that, man. I come in peace.' He seemed somewhat out of breath and more than a little apprehensive. He held up his arms to show he was unarmed.

'Who are you?' Jude shouted. 'And where do you come from?'

The man nodded and showed his white teeth. 'Name's Josh Appleseed. And I come seeking sanctuary.'

'Sanctuary?' Jude repeated. He knew full well what sanctuary meant, but he was surprised to hear a black man using the term.

'Yes, sanctuary,' the man said. 'Like if those scumbags catch up on me they'll most probably string me up for a horse thief.'

'Why would they do that?' Jude asked him.

'That's because I stole a horse,' the man said with brutal frankness, 'and a saddle too.'

Jude looked beyond him but saw no sign of other riders. 'You mean they're on your trail right now?'

The man showed his teeth again. 'They're not too far off, you can bet on that.'

Jude took a gamble. He lowered his gun and gestured to the man. 'Get off that horse of yours and come right on in. As long as you come in peace there's nothing to be worried about.'

'Thanks, man,' Josh Appleseed said. He dismounted and tethered his horse to the fence and walked towards Jude. Jude saw that he was quite tall and well muscled and he moved with a kind of easy grace that Jude had not seen in any white man he knew.

Jude looked him straight in the eye and figured he had an honest face. People were like horses in that respect: if a horse was honest and good it had a friendly look in its eye; if it was suspicious, or had been treated badly, it had a baleful suspicious look in its eye. 'I guess you must be hungry and thirsty,' he said.

Josh nodded slowly. 'I could sure use a bite and at least a gallon of water,' he said. 'But that poor dumb beast I stole has been through hell and high-water and he needs his nourishment too. So maybe we could fix him up first.'

Jude was glad to hear that. He liked to treat his horses well because he figured they always paid you back in kind. 'Well, we haven't got much here, mister, but you and your horse are welcome to what we do have. So take your horse to the drinking trough and then put it in the barn so it can stoke up on that good hay we've got.'

Josh Appleseed smiled and took a slightly mocking bow. 'Well, thank you kindly for that. And please don't call me mister. It makes me feel a tad uneasy. I'm just Josh or Appleseed.'

'And I'm just Jude or James.'

Josh Appleseed grinned. 'Jude James. That has a good ring to it. So I reckon I'll call you Jude or Mr James.'

'And I'll call you Josh or Mr Appleseed. That has a wholesome ring about it.'

After they'd attended to Josh Appleseed's horse they went inside the cabin and Josh looked around somewhat warily. 'You live alone here?' he asked.

'I don't have no womenfolk, if that's what you mean. And

since my ma and pa died, I don't have any kin either.'

'I'm right sorry to hear that, man,' Josh Appleseed declared and, though he was still smiling, something deep in his eyes reflected a kind of enduring melancholy.

'And you don't need to worry,' Jude said, 'because we don't have mantraps in here. So just sit yourself down and we'll eat what we have. There isn't much. Just cornbread and a small haunch of deer I have. It might be a bit ripe, but I guess we'll survive. And I do happen to have coffee and even a little home brew.'

'That sounds wonderful,' Josh said. 'Indeed, I'm most grateful, Mr James.'

They sat down at the table across from one another and Jude served out the food. He wondered if he was being a damned fool but there was something about this man Josh Appleseed he felt he could trust, a kind of openheartedness you had to warm to. And Josh Appleseed sure was hungry. He devoured his food, simple as it was, as though he was stocking up for the crack of doom.

When he'd finished he reached for his bandanna and cleaned his mouth. 'Used to have a whole bunch of these,' he said, 'but I'm afraid my manners have slipped away somewhat.'

Jude was impressed. Josh Appleseed had obviously seen better days.

Josh seemed to read his thoughts. 'I can see by the way you look at me that you wonder where I dropped in from and who I really am.'

'That had crossed my mind,' Jude agreed, 'since you have the ways of someone who is almost a gentleman.'

'Almost is a long hop,' Josh laughed. 'But since you took me in like the Good Samaritan – or was that the inn keeper? – I guess I should tell you something about myself.'

And so he told his story.

*

Appleseed had been a slave, the son of slaves in the South. His mother and father had been sold into slavery half a century before. Both had worked in the cotton fields and they were lucky enough to have a humane master who treated them well. Eventually, they had been promoted to house slaves and, when Josh was born, he was taught with the master's own sons and daughters and then trained as a footman and later as the master's personal servant.

'He was a good and generous man,' Josh said, 'and he liked to discuss matters of mutual interest with me. We talked more as friends than as master and slave. He even told me that one day I would be free.'

Then came the war and the end of slavery ... well, officially, at least. During the war, Unionist soldiers invaded from the North and burned the old mansion to the ground. Josh's master had been shot down by a Unionist lieutenant and his wife and children had fled. Then Josh's life turned upside down completely. He had never agreed with slavery, but at least he had a good master and a comfortable life. Now he had great difficulty in finding work and the conditions of his life went down almost to zero. Eventually he had been offered a job by a man called Andrew Mcdee but the wages had been so poor that he might just as well have been a slave again.

'Mcdee!' Jude said. 'So you worked for him?'

'I slaved for him!' Josh exclaimed. 'That man would cut a pound of flesh from your poor aching body and not think twice about it.'

'So you must know Maddock and his two sidekicks!'

'Not only do I know them, I've come upon them fist to fist. A few days ago those two boys roughed me up a little and I've got the bruises to prove it. That's why I made my big decision

21

to cut loose. So, I purloined that good horse out there and the harness with it. I figured Mcdee owed me since he almost drained the life blood right out of my body.'

Jude looked him over. He didn't look too lean. In fact, as he had noticed earlier the man looked well muscled and healthy. 'How d'you keep yourself in shape?' he asked.

'Well, what would you do? I stole food and I became indeed quite a good food thief. My ma and pa would be proud of me, not for my thieving but for my prowess in doing it.'

Jude thought that over for a while. 'So what do you aim to do now?' he asked.

Josh creased his brow. 'I don't rightly know, but I do know one thing: if I hang around here for too long those scumbags are going to catch up with me and then there'll be hell to pay. So I'm going to ride off into the sunset and leave you in peace.'

'Well, now,' Jude said after a moment's thought, 'as it happens I'm in deep trouble myself with that man Mcdee and his agent, that poisonous *hombre* Maddock. So, I'm on the point of leaving myself.'

'Well, isn't that something!' Josh said in astonishment. 'So, why don't we ride along together, that's if you're not colour blind?'

'It's not the colour of a man's skin that you judge him by,' Jude said, 'it's what lies under his skin. So I think we could team up and ride out of here together. What do you think about that, Mr Appleseed?'

Josh Appleseed's face beamed. 'I think that would be just fine, Mr James.'

Jude gathered all he needed together: the cornbread, the rest of the haunch of deer, as much of the home-brew as he could carry in his canteen, a bedroll, and a small tent, and a few other items of clothing.

'What will you do with the rest?' Josh asked.

'If you can see anything you take a fancy to, bring it along with you.'

'Well, that's real kind of you,' Josh said. 'If you got a shirt to spare, I'd appreciate it and that's just about all.' He looked around the cabin. 'What about the rest, the chairs and table, and the other items;

'I've thought about that,' Jude said, 'and I've come up with a solution.'

'And what would that be?'

'I reckon I'm going to have a funeral pyre,' Jude said.

Josh looked startled. 'You mean like burn the place down?'

Jude nodded. 'It seems like—'

—'appropriate,' Josh prompted.

'You sure have the gift of words,' Jude told him.

'How else would I have survived in this crazy old world, man?' Josh laughed.

When they had everything they needed together it was almost sundown, time to hit the hay, quite literally since they decided it might be dangerous to sleep in the cabin; Maddock and his two sidekicks might sneak up on them. So it would be better to sleep out in the barn with the horses.

'Sleeping with the horses isn't something new to me,' Josh said. 'One time I was treated no better than a horse myself. In fact, I was treated a lot worse than the beasts in the field by Mcdee and his sidekick Maddock.'

Come sunup they ate their tuck and got ready to ride out. Fortunately, the weather was fine and it was early June. Maddock and his men hadn't shown yet, but Jude figured it wouldn't be long.

'Pity we've only got one gun between us,' Josh said. 'That means one of us is without means of defence.'

'Well, now you come to mention it,' Jude said. 'We do have another gun. It's a Remington twelve gauge shotgun. Could be quite effective if you cared to bring it along. You ever used one before?'

'Never fired a shot in anger,' Josh said. 'Never wanted to. But I might be tempted by Mcdee or Maddock, not to mention those two gun-toting hell raisers of his.'

'Well, bring the shotgun along and hope you don't need to use it. My pa told me it could be useful at close quarters. "Could spatter a man to hell", he said, though I never had the misfortune to try it out myself and I hope I never need to.'

'Then we'll take it along just in case we need to do just that,' Josh said.

Jude chased one of the hens and wrung its neck. After that he collected the eggs. 'We've got enough to feed us for a week,' he said.

'What will you do with the stock?' Josh asked.

'We drive them off and hope they'll take care of themselves,' Jude said.

Josh nodded thoughtfully. 'You really mean to burn the place down?'

'Why not?' Jude said. 'If you lean against it too hard it will fall over, anyway.'

'I think it might not be good sense to do that burning, man.'

'Why not?'

'Because it's a waste of energy and time. While we're leaping around the flames enjoying ourselves, those scaramouches might ride up and take us unawares. Who wants to see two dead men roasting like chestnuts in a fire?'

Jude held up a finger. 'You got a point there, Mr Appleseed.

A man can get over excited. So we'll just ride out nice and easy and hope for a brighter future somewhere over the horizon. Is that what we should do?'

'That's the best thing,' Josh conceded. 'Pity we can't take the cows along with us. Maybe we could sell them off to a local farmer?'

'That's not such a good plan, Mr Appleseed. The cows would slow us down too much, and those skookums might catch up on us a little too easily.'

'Good thinking, partner.' Josh held up his hand and Jude slapped his palm against it. Then they urged their mounts forward and rode off in a westerly direction.

'Where are we headed?' Josh asked.

'I have no exact notion,' Jude said. 'We don't need to push the horses too hard. Thirty miles could be enough for one day.'

'Best to follow the river west. That way we'll hit the trail sooner or later,' Josh suggested.

They jogged on west letting the horses set their own pace. At first it was nice and easy. They passed homesteads where people waved to them and called out greetings. Then gradually the farmsteads thinned out and they were on their own in a deepening wilderness.

'I guess we should rest the horses here and let them graze a little. There's a creek where they could take a refreshing drink too,' Jude suggested.

'Good thinking, man.'

So they reined in and dismounted.

'How far d'you reckon we've come?' Josh asked, surveying the undulating landscape.

'No more than fifteen miles, I guess,' Jude replied.

They hobbled the horses and let them graze along the

river-bank under the shadow of the squat oaks where there was an abundance of grass. The two horses seemed quite at ease and companionable and grateful for the rest.

Josh lay back and closed his eyes. Then he opened them again. 'You hear what I hear?' he asked Jude.

Jude screwed up his eyes and listened. In the distance he could hear the baying of a dog. He looked at Josh. 'I hear a dog howling.'

Josh was already getting to his feet. 'That's no ordinary dog. That's Mcdee's hunting dog and he's coming our way.'

'That means trouble,' Jude said. 'You set a hunting dog on a man he will find him. A dog has a sense of smell a hundred times better than a man's, or maybe even more. I didn't think Mcdee and Maddock would be so—'

'—vindictive,' Josh prompted again.

'You got it,' Jude agreed. 'The question is what do we do now?'

'What we do is we take cover in this stand of trees and wait for the inevitable. And my advice would be to cock that shooter of yours and hold it ready because those skookums mean business and it isn't just a matter of handing loose change over a counter.'

So they took cover among the oaks and waited and they didn't have to wait long. That baying hound came closer and closer until they could see the dog lolloping along with its snarling fangs exposed.

'Here he comes,' Josh said quietly, 'and those gun-toting scaramouches won't be too far behind.'

'Sounds like that hound is enjoying the chase,' Jude said.

'Oh, he's enjoying it right enough,' Josh agreed. 'He's a real man-eater, that one.'

The next moment the dog was plunging among the trees snarling at them as though they were no more than pieces of meat dripping with blood! But instead of leaping at Jude's throat, it checked and just pointed its nose towards Jude and seemed to wait. Jude heard the hoofbeats against the ground as the riders closed in for the kill.

He pointed the Colt at the dog's head and pulled the trigger. 'Don't pull, squeeze,' he heard his father say, but it was too late. It worked, anyway. The dog leaped right up in the air and dropped down like a stone.

'Good shooting!' Josh said from close beside him. 'Now you've got five more rounds and you're going to need every last one.'

Jude cocked the pistol and saw the two riders riding towards them. Now they were real close, close enough to recognize. One of them was Maddock and the other was one of his henchmen. Where was the third one? Jude wondered.

There was no time for much thinking. Maddock was levelling his gun and getting ready to fire.

'Hold your fire and take cover,' Josh advised from close by. 'A man on horseback is likely to be a little unsteady in his aim. Make those five shots count.'

Jude crouched down behind a tree and steadied himself. Killing the dog had been strangely unnerving but he knew it might be a matter of kill or be killed.

Maddock shouted something and then fired his weapon. The bullet whined in close to Jude's head but it was meant to kill.

'Keep steady!' Josh warned. 'Those varmints want to flush us out so they can kill us.' Jude felt an unfamiliar tingle in his spine. So they really want to kill us! he thought. But there was no time to feel afraid because the next moment Josh put his hand on his shoulder. 'Keep still and steady,' he said. 'That missing henchman is stealing round to the horses. I think he wants to run them off so they can pick us off more easily.'

Jude just nodded and looked out at Maddock and his henchman. They were wheeling round on their horses and trying to make up their minds what to do. Make every shot count, he thought as Josh slid away towards the horses.

Then Maddock shouted out again. 'Are you coming out, or are we coming in to get you!'

'Don't waste your breath,' Jude said to himself as he peered round the trunk of tree. He heard the whinnying of a horse from the direction of the creek and then there was a loud bang followed by another as the Remington shotgun was discharged.

'My God, you killed me!' a voice shouted in horror.

'Don't be distracted,' Jude said to himself. He looked out towards Maddock and his sidekick and saw that a sudden change had come over them. It was as if the courage had been sucked from their bones.

The two riders backed their horses off a piece. Then Maddock shouted again. 'So you killed one of my men and my dog!' he said brazenly. 'You think you've won this round but I tell you this: think again because you won't be thinking much in future. You might consider you're safe, but you better watch your back because we're coming in to get you wherever you happen to be and you won't know when it's gonna happen, you hear me?'

'Don't answer,' Josh said from beside him. 'We've got them rattled. Lucky we found the right place to rest up. If they'd caught us out in the open it might have been a very different story.'

Jude turned to see Josh's teeth flashing. 'That Remington shotgun did a whole lot better than I expected. That poor guy was blown right apart.'

CHAPTER THREE

Jude looked down at the dead man and almost felt sorry for him. It was one of Mcdee's hard-faced thugs but now there was an expression of horror on his face as though he couldn't believe what had happened to him. He was peppered with shot from that Remington shotgun.

'That was no saintly passing,' Josh said. 'Must have thought he was invincible right up till the last breath. I hope he saw the shining light, but I doubt it. But lookee here.'

Jude looked down and saw that the would-be killer was still clutching his revolver.

'Well, he won't need this any longer where he's going,' Josh reflected. He knelt down and prised the weapon from the man's hand and held it up. 'This is a Colt Peacemaker same as yours,' he said. 'I think I might just keep it as a trophy.' He laid the revolver on the ground and rolled the dead man over. 'Cartridge belt and holster too. He won't need any of this. I guess there's no shooting in heaven or the other place. But there might be a few devils with toasting forks to prod you with, though I guess a shooter wouldn't be too useful against them either.' He unbuckled the man's gunbelt and rolled the body away.

'So you aren't superstitious?' Jude asked him.

'Well,' Josh said, 'I can sing a few hymns and recite a few prayers, but no, I guess I'm not superstitious.' He held up the gunbelt and inspected it. There's a drop of blood splashed here and there but I can wash that off.' He went down to the creek and washed blood off into the flowing water. 'And lookee here,' he said, shaking the water off. 'That's the man's horse unless I'm mistaken. Seems to have taken a shine to ours. So, maybe we should take him along with us too, just to be companionable.' He stood up and strapped the gunbelt around his waist. 'Fits just right,' he said. 'He was a little tighter around the middle than me but I can notch it up a piece.' He retrieved the Colt Peacemaker from the ground and slid it into the holster. 'Fits snug and neat,' he said. 'I just hope it doesn't have a curse on it.'

'I think we should mount up and ride out of here,' Jude suggested. 'Those two skookums aren't going to be too pleased they failed in their mission and, when they go back to Mcdee without our scalps, he won't be too happy either.'

'That's good thinking too, Mr James,' Josh agreed.

So they saddled their horses and mounted up taking the dead man's horse along with them.

They rode steadily west until the sun was beginning to roll away like a ball of red fire behind the trees.

'Just like a big hot face sweating with joy,' Josh pronounced. 'I've seen it a thousand times and it never ceases to amaze me. There has to be something out there so beautiful you could scarcely believe it if you rode right off the earth and into the sky. Have you ever thought about that, Mr James?'

'I've seen it and I've been amazed by it too, but right now I reckon we should think about pitching camp somewhere.'

'Guess you're right,' Josh said. 'We've been following the creek all afternoon, I guess it shouldn't be too difficult.'

So they dismounted and hobbled the horses close to the water. Josh conjured up a fire and Jude got out his small tent and erected it.

'I see you brought along your tent,' Josh observed. 'That's really fancy, man.'

'Just an old army tent my pa had,' Jude said. 'Enough room for two men inside.'

'So you don't mind sleeping in a two-man tent with a black man?' Josh chuckled.

'Black or white, it won't make a whole lot of difference in the dark unless a man snores.'

'I guess I wouldn't care too much if a man snores because I've learned to sleep like one of those dead knights of old in the stories. Just one thing though, Mr James.'

'And what's that, Mr Appleseed?'

'How about if those skookums creep up on us during the night?'

Jude considered for a moment. 'Well, unless you want to take turns on watch I think we'll have to take a chance on that.'

Josh nodded. 'I reckon so. Though I sleep deep I can wake as quick as any bird. And something seems to tell me those bully boys won't be coming at us for more of the same treatment.'

They sat by the fire and ate what they had which wasn't a whole lot.

'Tell you something,' Josh said. 'Sooner or later we're going to have to get us some supplies, you know that?'

Jude nodded. 'Well, I've thought on that too and I reckon we have two choices.'

'And what would those two choices be?' Josh asked him.

Jude inclined his head with a grin. 'Either we look for honest work, or we steal. I can't think of a third way, can you?'

31

Josh gave his usual broad smile. 'I don't like to put labels on myself, but if it comes to crisis point I've had a deal of experience at thieving and I might say I'm an expert at it. But on balance I think I prefer the honest way. So I guess we should look for some kind of genuine work.'

'I'm inclined to agree on that,' Jude said with a hint of irony.

By good fortune nothing happened to disturb them through the night other than the howl of coyotes just before sunset and again at dawn.

'Those critters sure know when it's time to hit the hay and rise up again,' Josh said, as he fried eggs in a pan for breakfast. 'They know a whole lot more about how to live than we do. I guess when all the people have gone from the face of the earth they'll still be around howling and mating and wreaking havoc.'

Early morning wasn't Jude's best thinking time so he concentrated on eating his eggs. Josh did them over and easy so they were cooked evenly on both sides. His cooking skills were almost refined.

'Tell you something, Mr Appleseed,' Jude said after a while.

Josh grinned. 'What's that, Mr James?'

'We hit the right spot you could take a job as a cook. How would you like that?'

'I'd like that fine, man. But what about you? What would you do?'

Jude shrugged. 'I'll think of something. Maybe I could learn about the art of cookery too.'

Josh shrugged. 'Nothing to it. If you're partial to your food, you can learn to cook. If you just choke food down to keep yourself from starving you're never going to learn. It's as simple as that.'

As they sat there by the fire eating they suddenly heard sounds, the pounding of hoofs and the jingle of harness.

'I think we've got company,' Josh said. 'Maybe those skookums are coming in to shoot us up again.'

They got to their feet and drew their Peacemakers. Then they stood close to the aspens so they wouldn't be too conspicuous. Looking out they saw six riders coming towards them. They were riding in a leisurely fashion as though they were in no particular hurry to get anywhere. One thing was certain: they weren't Mcdee's men. Neither Josh nor Jude had seen them before.

The riders drew closer and one of them held up his hand. 'No need for shooters, my friends,' he said in a deep melodious voice. 'We don't mean no harm. We're just wayfarers like you.'

Wayfarers, Jude thought. Those *hombres* are well tooled up for wayfarers. He noted that the men all wore gunbelts with revolvers and they had carbines in saddle holsters too. Somehow the word wayfarers didn't seem exactly right. He glanced at Josh and saw by his expression that he was equally wary.

The leader of the group wore a wide-brimmed Stetson that partly hid his face, so it was difficult to read what he was thinking, or what his intentions might be. Yet his deep voice had been amiable enough. The other members of the band were varied in appearance. Two were dark and might have been Mexican, and one had long wavy hair like a Nordic chief. The other two could have been of Italian or Spanish extraction. It was impossible to tell.

'We're just about to go on our way,' Jude said.

'Yeah, breaking camp,' Josh added.

The man in the wide-brimmed Stetson grinned. 'In that case we won't be bothering you none,' he said. He dismounted and

33

walked forward with his arm extended. Jude took the proffered hand and the man squeezed his hand tightly. 'Name's
Nolan,' he said. 'Brod Nolan. Maybe you've heard of me?'

The name meant nothing to Jude. 'Good morning, Mr
Nolan. My name's Jude.'

Nolan's eyes switched to Josh. 'Is this your slave?' he asked.

'This is my friend.' Jude replied.

Nolan nodded and grinned, but he didn't offer his hand to
Josh.

The other five riders dismounted.

'Mind if we take advantage of your fire?' the one with the
long flowing hair said, in a strange sniggering sounding voice.

'We'd be glad to share it with you,' Jude said.

The riders took their mounts to the creek and let them
drink their fill.

'You had your chuck?' Nolan said in a friendly tone.

'As I said we're about to pull out,' Josh told him.

'Which way are you riding?' Nolan asked.

'Generally due west,' Jude said. 'We're looking for work of
some kind.'

Nolan gave Josh a searching look. 'Have you been a slave,
man?'

Josh grinned pleasantly. 'I would describe myself more as a
servant,' he said.

'Well,' Nolan said, 'you sure know how to use the English
language. Where did you pick that up?'

Josh continued grinning. 'I was a house servant to a
wealthy family, but now I'm free to do as I please.'

That gave rise to more laughter, but Jude noticed it was
slightly more restrained as though some of the band thought
Josh might have adopted a slightly jeering tone. Men who
spoke well often had that effect, especially if they happened
to be black.

But when Nolan spoke again, he was still smiling. 'What do they call you?' he asked.

Josh shrugged. 'I've been called a whole heap of things,' he replied.

'I bet you have,' the man with the long blond hair said. 'And I can guess what some of them might be.'

Josh decided to ignore that remark. 'Name's Josh,' he told Nolan. 'Josh Appleseed.'

'Appleseed,' one of the men put in. 'That's a real strange name.

'Strange or not,' Josh replied, 'that's what they call me.'

'I thought it might Jimbo or Darky,' the other man said.

The rest of the gang laughed heartily. They obviously weren't gifted with a refined sense of humour.

'Well now, boys, why don't we polish up on our manners?' Nolan said. He turned to Josh. 'So you're a man of some skill,' he said.

Josh nodded. 'I've learned a few things in my time, Mr Nolan. That's what life is about, I believe.'

Nolan chuckled. 'Then why don't you two boys team up with us for a while if you have nothing better to do?'

Josh and Jude exchanged glances and Jude nodded. 'We could ride along with you for a while, that's if you're going our way. Maybe you could tell us what your line of business is?'

There was moment's silence and then the members of the bunch all burst out laughing, Nolan even more loudly than the rest. 'What we do,' he said, 'what we do is we live on our wits. It's surprising what you can come up with when you live on your wits. You should try it some time.'

There was another murmur of laughter from the boys.

The man with the long hair said, 'Mister Brod Nolan here owns a whole chunk of a town further west from here.'

'Is that so,' Josh said.

'We could ride along with you for a mile or two,' Jude agreed.

Josh raised his eyebrows and said nothing.

They mounted up and rode along together for a while. Jude glanced at Josh and saw by his expression that he wanted to say something, but Josh kept his peace and just hummed to himself. Nolan rode beside them, so it was difficult to talk without being overheard.

'See you brought along a spare horse,' Nolan said after a while.

Josh looked at Jude and still said nothing.

'We thought it would be good to have a spare horse with us,' Jude said.

'Spare saddle too,' Nolan said, 'and unless my eyes deceive me, a spare carbine. That could be useful.'

'We're pessimists, Mr Nolan,' Josh said at last. 'A man can't be too well prepared in the wilderness.'

'Too true, too true,' Nolan acknowledged, with his eyes on the spare mount. 'What d'you call the beast?'

Josh chuckled. 'We don't call him anything, man,' he said. 'He's just horse to us.'

The man with the long blond hair laughed again in his slightly jeering fashion. 'A horse is a horse is a horse. Is that what you're saying?'

'We don't talk about it a whole lot,' Josh said. Jude saw by the way he glanced in his direction that Josh was feeling some-what uneasy, and he obviously didn't care much for the guy with the long hair.

'Where are we headed?' Jude asked Nolan.

Nolan raised his head and sniffed the air. 'Around thirty miles off, we've got a little place tucked away behind a stand of trees. Not much but we use it as a base. A kind of centre of operations if you understand me.' He gave Jude a shrewd look and half closed one eye.

A base for operations, Jude thought. *What operations would those be?* A vague thought had been buzzing like a lazy bee around in his mind and now it suddenly struck him right on the forehead. The word *Nolan* lit up and he remembered he had seen a poster in town with the name Brod Nolan on it. BROD NOLAN WANTED FOR ARMED ROBBERY. And there had been a reward offered too. Jude couldn't remember how much.

Jude looked at Josh again and Josh inclined his head. A kind of stiffness had crept over him, a wariness that suggested that he knew about Brod Nolan too.

They rode on through the day without much conversation, except for the members of the gang who spoke mostly in Spanish which neither Jude nor Josh could understand. Long Hair obviously understood it and he laughed from time to time in his rather sinister, high-pitched tone. Jude had a strange feeling that he and Josh were prisoners under escort. But why had the Nolan gang decided to bring them along?

Part of the answer came after they had been riding for an hour and several long low cabins came into view.

'That's what passes for home,' Nolan said. 'You boys let those horses of yours take a drink and a bite of hay and then come right in and make yourselves snug and comfortable. You might even have yourselves a bath if Nancy has lit up the range.'

As they dismounted, a grey-haired man of around fifty appeared in the doorway holding a shotgun.

'Hi, Jake!' Nolan greeted. 'I see you brought out the artillery to welcome us.'

The grey-haired man nodded and gave a grin. 'Can't be too careful, Mr Nolan. Never know who's prowling around in those woods up there.'

'That is so,' Nolan said with a chuckle. 'As you see we brought in two wayfarers. This here is Jude. And this dark man is called Josh. I believe he's an expert cook and he's looking for work in that field.'

'That's good,' the older man said, nodding at the two strangers. 'Nancy will be glad of help with the chow. She's real good in the cooking department, but you can't have too many hands with such a large bunch of hungry men.'

Jude noticed that old Jake didn't laugh though the flicker of a smile crossed his visage occasionally like pale moonshine peeping from behind a rather dense cloud.

As soon as they stepped inside the cabin the woman Nancy appeared and she wasn't what Jude had expected at all. He had pictured a grey-haired, oldish woman who was probably Jake's wife, but Nancy was no more than twenty-two, he reckoned, and might have been good looking if she was given a smart dress and was spruced up a bit.

'This is my daughter Nancy,' Jake said. 'She does most of the work around here.'

Nancy gave Jude a slightly suspicious look and a bob and Jude took her hand which was surprisingly small and delicate considering all the work she had to do.

'And this here is Josh,' Nolan introduced.

Josh gave Nancy one of his gleaming smiles and then bowed like a gentleman meeting a foreign dignitary.

'Now why don't we all go through and take our rest?' Nolan invited. He was obviously like a king in this establishment.

They all went through to what they called the long room and sat around as though waiting for someone to serve them a meal. Most of them lit up quirlies or filled their pipes and soon the room was bluish and hazy with smoke, which nobody seemed to mind.

There was a barrel at the end of the room and Nancy and Jake started handing out mugs of a foaming liquid Nolan said was beer. 'This is the Nancy special,' he said. 'A pint will knock you right off your feet. Ain't that so, boys?'

'Sure is,' Long Hair said, puffing away at his curly pipe. 'Can't get enough of it myself.'

There was a hoot of approval from the rest of the gang.

Jude sniffed his beer suspiciously and Josh raised his eyebrows as if to say, 'Drink this swill and you'll be right out cold before you can count to three!'

Nancy smiled a rather sweet smile. 'Don't worry, it won't kill you. It'll just relax you a little. That's why the boys like it so much.'

'Sure, that's why we like it,' Long Hair agreed.

Jude sipped his drink and found it had a strong cheesy flavour. Josh held it in his mouth and then at the back of his throat before swallowing it down.

'Don't worry, that ain't Injun juice,' Long Hair warned. 'You know what happens to Injuns when they taste that stuff. They go stark raving crazy.'

'I thought that was moonshine,' Josh said with a polite smile.

Long Hair leaned towards him with a sneer. 'I heard it was the same with you. You think that's true?'

Jude noticed a slight tightening of Josh's jaw, but Josh was still smiling. 'I wouldn't know about that.'

Long Hair gave his usual unpleasant chuckle. 'I think we've got a bottle of rye somewhere hereabouts. Maybe you should try it later, see if what they say is true.'

Josh was still smiling. 'I think I'll pass on that, mister.'

Jude felt tension like an over-strung wire between Josh and Long Hair. Long Hair was obviously a man who enjoyed a quarrel and hated men of colour and his voice had a drawl which might indicate that he was from a slave-owning family from the south. So he felt some relief when Nancy and her father started to dish out the supper. There were gobbets of meat of some kind and a few root vegetables cooked in a thin gravy. Though it wasn't fancy it was, at least, edible and the boys tucked into it with relish. Their table manners were somewhat lacking, except for Brod Nolan's who ate with a certain degree of delicacy.

'Well, we seem to have a couple of real high-class dudes here,' Long Hair mocked after wiping his mouth on his sleeve. 'Where d'you learn those fancy manners, boys?' He was leering in the direction of Jude and Josh who were sitting together.

Though Josh was still smiling politely, Jude felt the wire tightening.

'We didn't learn them,' he said to calm things down. 'It just came sort of naturally.'

Long Hair gave his jeering laugh and a wary silence fell on the room. Clearly he was a man with a pile of wood chips on his right shoulder. 'So you're a slave lover, are you?' he demanded.

Jude felt a strange prickling sensation at the back of his neck. It was the feeling he experienced just before he was about to take a swing at a man who had insulted his pa and ma. 'What I love is personal,' he said. 'But what I hate is when a friend is abused.'

That gave rise to a murmur of what might have been approval or disapproval round the table.

Jude picked up his mug and took a swig of his cheesy beer.

Long Hair rose from his stool and, though he was grinning, there was a look of pure fury in his eyes. 'Are you insulting me, boy?'

Jude placed his mug on the table and looked at Long Hair. The man was tall, maybe six feet or so, and he was muscular, and he was raring for a fight. Jude glanced at Josh and then slowly rose to his feet.

But before he could speak, Josh rose as well. 'I don't think there's any insulting intended here,' he said quietly. 'It's just that you don't care for black men and black men don't care too much for you. So, if there's an issue here it's between you and me and not between you and my friend.'

Long Hair took a deep breath and turned towards Josh. 'Well, I've never had the need to whip a black man before but there's a first time for everything. So maybe you and me should step outside.'

Josh nodded slowly. 'Maybe we should,' he said.

Jude wanted to put a restraining hand on Josh's shoulder, but before he could move, Nolan raised his mug and brought it down like a mace on the table. 'OK, boys,' he said, 'I think we should calm down before things get out of hand. We've all had quite a long day and it's time to rest up.'

One of the Mexicans piped up. 'You're right there, boss. Maybe Nancy can sing one of those beautiful lullabies she's so good at and we can all smoke our pipes and listen.'

That met with a mixed response. Some of the boys were obviously itching to see a fight and even place bets on the result, but other more cool heads were only too pleased to see peace return. Long Hair was still looking furious but he sat down and held up his mug to be refilled and Nancy duly obliged. Then he sat down and turned to his neighbour and said something soto voce Jude could hear perfectly well: 'That bastard and his black-loving sidekick ain't seen nothing yet. I would have smashed both their heads in for them.'

His companion growled his assent.

*

41

After the meal Nancy approached Jude and Josh. 'Why don't you follow me, boys, and I'll show you to your cabin.'

Jude had noticed that there were several cabins on the spread but he had assumed they would all sleep in the same bunkhouse together. Nancy led them to a smaller cabin which had obviously been used as a store.

'Mr Nolan has asked me to put you in here,' she said, opening the door and holding her lantern above her head so that they could see into the room. 'I'll leave the lantern for you, so you can see your way around.'

'Thanks a lot, Nancy,' Josh smiled. 'Tell me two things: first, why are we here on our own and not in the bunkhouse, and the second, what is a nice girl like you doing in a Godforsaken place like this, anyway?'

They were now inside the cabin where there were two bunks and a row of store cupboards. The place smelled of sawdust and some kind of indefinable oil, but at least it was clean.

'The answer to the first question is that Mr Nolan thinks this is the best place for you in case of trouble.'

'You mean trouble with that guy with the long hair and the big mouth?' Josh laughed.

'It's no laughing matter,' the girl said. 'He likes to pick on other men. His name's Jed Oliphant and he's a real killer at heart. You should beware of him because he might want to kill you.'

'Is that so?' Josh laughed. 'So what's the answer to the other question?'

'You mean, why am I here?'

Josh nodded. 'Somehow you don't seem to fit in.'

Nancy sighed. 'My pa and me were destitute and Brod Nolan took pity on us, but that's a long story.'

Josh gave her a look of concern. 'Does that mean you're

Nolan's woman?' he asked, somewhat tactlessly.

Nancy gave a wan smile. 'I'm everyone's woman,' she replied sadly.

After Nancy had left them, the two men laid their bedrolls on their bunks and got ready to turn in for the night.

'Well, Mr James, what do you think? Have we had a happy day?' Josh asked Jude.

'Well, Mr Appleseed,' Jude replied, 'I should say we've had not so much a happy day as an interesting one.'

'The question that's troubling me is should we stay or should we light out before we get deeper into the do-do?' Josh asked.

'What's your opinion on that, Mr Appleseed?' Jude said.

Josh inclined his head and considered. 'Well, one thing's for sure: if we stay and throw in our lot with this bunch, sooner or later one of us will need to punch the daylights out of that long-haired bastard because we won't have any peace if we don't.'

'I'm inclined to agree with that,' Jude said. 'Maybe we should toss a coin to see who has the privilege of doing it.'

'I think we should let Mother Nature decide. I figure she won't take long to make up her mind.' Josh frowned. 'But there's another consideration floating around in the deep recesses of my mind.'

'And what's that?'

Josh paused for a moment. 'I'm thinking of that young woman Nancy. There's something not right here and that's for sure.'

Jude ran his hand over his bristly chin. 'Well, Mr Appleseed, we can't be expected to put all the wrongs of the world to rights, can we?'

Josh paused to consider again. 'Well, that's correct, Mr

James, but when a problem passes right under our nose, I think that gives us the challenge of solving it. Wouldn't you agree?'

Jude grinned. 'I think we must think about that one in the morning when our minds are clearer,' he said. 'In the meantime, it might be best to lay our heads on what passes for pillows here and close our eyes and let nature take its course.'

CHAPTER FOUR

They woke to the sound of cockcrow and, after a moment, someone pushed open the door and stuck his head in. It was the old man Jake. With the light shining behind him he looked like Saint Joseph himself.

'You boys up and ready?' he asked laconically.

'We're almost on our feet,' Josh replied, as he swung out of his cot.

'Well, late risers don't get much of a look in here,' the old man said, 'that is as far as breakfast is concerned. If you aim to eat you'd better get your heads under the pump and freshen up before all the hard tack is gobbled up by those greedy son-of-a-guns out there.' Then the old man disappeared without closing the door and a thin blade of cold air knifed into the room.

'Just like home,' Josh chuckled, as he pulled on his pants and dragged on his boots.

Jude got up a little more slowly and did the same. Outside it was fresh and they located the pump quickly enough as two of the Spanish-speaking *hombres* stood pouring water over each other from leather buckets.

'I don't feel quite ready for a dousing,' Josh announced.

'That's something we can both agree on,' Jude said. 'You

got any soap, Mr Appleseed?'

'Indeed, that's something I do have,' Josh said, as he lathered himself down. He threw the soap at Jude who caught it neatly and followed his example.

'You feel fresh and lively as a cricket?' Josh asked him.

Jude was trying not to shiver as he dried himself on a prickly towel.

'Reminds me of my days of servitude,' Josh said, putting on his shirt and his over garments.

They walked together towards the main building where they saw Long Hair Oliphant waiting for them at the door. Long Hair grinned and nodded his head maliciously. 'You boys looking for breakfast I'm afraid you're gonna be disappointed because there's nothing left in the pan.'

'Well, we'll just take a peek inside if you'll be kind enough to stand aside,' Josh said.

Long Hair was standing right in the doorway like a fixed statue in a museum, and he showed no sign of moving. He looked at Josh with a sneer. 'I might think about it if you say, "Yes please, Master". Isn't that the way you're supposed to address the superior race?'

Josh was smiling but Jude saw no humour in the smile. He knew a fight was brewing, but he also knew that he couldn't intervene because it was a matter of honour between Josh and the bully. Then quite suddenly something completely unexpected occurred. Although Josh scarcely seemed to move, his fists shot out like pistons straight into Long Hair's midriff. Long Hair doubled up and his face made sudden contact with Josh's knee. He gasped and collapsed against the door post and slid towards the floor. Josh leaned over and dragged him to his feet. Then he bounced Long Hair's head against the door post and thrust him aside like a sack of grain.

'Please may I pass, master?' he said, in imitation of a mangy cur.

Long Hair didn't reply. He was too busy coughing up his breakfast on the ground.

Josh and Jude went on into the room and over to the table where Nancy was dolling out the breakfast.

'We hear there isn't a lot left,' Josh said. Though he was slightly out of breath he was calm enough.

Nancy looked at him and almost laughed. 'Did you kill him?' she asked.

'Not quite,' Josh said, 'but I will if I have to.'

'Then it's lucky I saved you your breakfast,' she said.

They carried their plates over to the long table and sat themselves down. There was silence in the room. The other hands were all staring in their direction but when they met their astonished gazes they all turned and lit their pipes or smoked their quirlies.

Jude looked across the table at Josh. 'Well, that was something,' he said. 'Where did you learn that, brother?'

Josh was biting into his biscuit. He grinned at Jude. 'You learn a lot when you're in servitude, Mr James. Like, if you don't learn, you end up at the bottom of the pile – or dead!'

They looked up and saw Brod Nolan staring down at them. 'I think we need to talk,' he said.

'Yes, sir,' Jude replied.

Nolan gave a ghost of a smile. 'Just as soon as you've had your chow, Nancy will show you where to find me. Then we can have a little exchange of views.' He turned and walked away out of the cabin, without stepping over Long Hair's body because Long Hair was no longer there.

Nancy was gathering up the tin plates and smiled nervously. 'I understand Mr Nolan wants to talk to you boys,' she said. 'If

47

you'll follow me I'll show you where is he is.'

Jude and Josh got to their feet, and Nancy was looking at Josh in particular. 'That was a brave thing to do, Mr Appleseed, but I hope you know what it might lead to.'

Josh flashed his white teeth. 'I know what revenge is, Miss Nancy. Indeed, I've seen a lot of it in my time.'

'Just as long as you remember that, Mr Appleseed.' Nancy smiled.

'I'll take good care to remember it, Miss Nancy.'

She led them across a yard where the hens were busy pecking up grain to another cabin where they found Nolan sitting behind a pile of crates that had been fashioned into some kind of desk.

'Sit you down, boys,' Nolan said, 'and we can have a little jawing session.'

Jude and Josh drew out crates and perched on them.

Nolan looked at Jude and then at Josh. 'Where did you learn that stuff?' he asked.

'What stuff is that, Mr Nolan?' Josh asked.

'The way you put down Jed Oliphant.'

Josh took a breath. 'As I said to my partner here, you learn a lot when you're in servitude. If you don't, you end up stiff and dead which no man aims for in my experience.'

Nolan nodded slowly and decisively as though what he had heard confirmed his suspicions. 'I think we have a slight difficulty here, Mr Appleseed.'

Josh showed his teeth again. 'I think we encountered that difficulty in the form of Oliphant on the way to breakfast, Mr Nolan.'

Nolan held his head on one side. 'The problem is I can't have bad blood between the men who ride with me. You understand what I'm saying to you?' He looked at Josh and then at Jude.

'Well, Mr Nolan, what you say is clear enough, but the question is, are we riding with you?' Jude said.

Nolan studied them for ten seconds and then pushed across a cigar box. 'Why don't you two boys smoke a cigar with me?'

Jude looked down at the box and saw the inscription Best Havana Cigars. 'Thanks a lot, Mr Nolan, but I don't think I can. You see they make me sick to my stomach.'

'And I never had chance to find out,' Josh said, 'since nobody ever offered me one before.'

Nolan gave a kind of grunting chuckle. 'Well, you boys certainly know your own minds and I respect that. So now I think I'd like to tell you about the outfit I run.'

'We'd both appreciate that, Mr Nolan,' Jude said.

Nolan sat back and relaxed. Then he took the cigar out of his mouth and exhaled a cloud of bluish smoke. Jude noticed he had a small, rather mean-looking mouth like a rat that has accidentally swallowed a plum stone.

'Well, boys,' he said, 'I work by instinct, but the moment I saw you by the river I had the distinct feeling you were the ones to ride with me. Call it some kind of superstition, if you like, but that hardly matters; it's the result that counts.'

Jude nodded and Josh blinked. 'I figure it depends what the result is,' Josh said, with an engaging smile.

Nolan grunted. 'That's what I like about you two boys; you've got heads screwed on to on your shoulders and you use them.'

'That's what they're there for, I understand, Mr Nolan,' Jude said.

Nolan leaned forward on his crate of a desk. 'You ever heard of William Clarke Quantrill?' he asked.

'I've heard of Quantrill's Raiders,' Jude said.

'Well, I was one of them at one time,' Nolan said. 'I rode

with Colonel Quantrill and his men. They included the James brothers, Jesse and Frank, and the Younger brothers, James and Bob. We were a pretty rough bunch back then.'

'I've heard of them too, Mr Nolan,' Jude said, 'but before you continue with your story I'd like to get one thing straight: I'm not related to the James brothers and I've never met them and never wanted to either.'

Nolan waved his cigar in the air. 'I know that, Mr James, and in any case it doesn't make a bean of difference to me. Those Quantrill Raiders did a heap of terribly bad things and I did bad things too until I suddenly saw the light, in a manner of speaking.'

'So you saw the light, Mr Nolan,' Josh said. 'Does that mean you saw the pearly gates open or something?'

Nolan laughed. 'No, nothing like that, Mr Appleseed. I just started to see Quantrill was crazy, that's all.'

'How d'you mean, crazy?' Jude asked. 'There's stark raving mad, or just mildly off whack.'

Nolan laughed again and his laugh was like the edge of a saw that's having difficulty with a particularly hard tree. 'Like he enjoyed seeing men suffer, and not only men but women and children too. Indeed, I've experienced many terrible things, but when I saw the light I decided to break away from those so-called raiders, and here I am. . . .' He spread wide his hands and spilled ash from his cigar on to the floor of the cabin.

'Here you are, Mr Nolan,' Jude agreed, 'but where exactly is here?'

Nolan chuckled to himself. 'Did you ever hear about that famous Robin Hood character of legend on the other side of the big ocean?'

'Wasn't he some kind of English guy who led a band of rebels?' Jude said.

Nolan held up his cigar like a finger of doom. 'You got it,' he said. 'That's right. This small band of mine imposes justice in this barren land. We take what we need from the rich and give a helping hand to those who are on their knees.'

Jude and Josh exchanged glances.

'You mean you rob the rich to feed the poor?' Josh asked him.

Nolan held up his cigar again. It seemed he used it as a orchestral conductor uses a baton, or a fisherman uses a rod to land a fish. 'What I'm trying to do is bring peace and order to this lawless country,' he pronounced.

There was silence for five seconds. Jude and Josh exchanged glances again.

'Well, that is indeed a tall order, Mr Nolan,' Jude said.

'Especially since we have lawmen in the country,' Josh added.

'But are they effective, Mr Appleseed?' Nolan asked, waving his cigar again.

Josh smiled and Jude looked thoughtful. 'So what does that add up to, Mr Nolan?' he asked.

Nolan took a long pull at his cigar. 'Like I said earlier,' he continued, 'if I'm to achieve my aims, I need men like you to help me. So what do you think about that?'

'That's a mighty big mouthful to chew on, Mr Nolan. But what exactly is the deal?'

Nolan seemed pleased by the answer. He knocked the ash off the end of his cigar on to the floor and nodded with satisfaction. 'If you ride with me you get your meals and whatever bounty we come across. Everything we get we share equally between us.'

'That sounds reasonable,' Josh said. 'I just have two questions: when you say everything we get, how do we get it? The second question, does equal mean equal?'

Nolan nodded. 'Everything is equal shares except that I take an extra cut because I'm leader and I do the planning.'

Josh glanced at Jude and raised his eyebrow a fraction. 'Which brings us back to the first question,' he asked. 'How do we get what we get?'

Nolan gave an enigmatic grin. 'I'm afraid I can't be too precise on that point,' he said. 'You see it depends on the circumstances.'

'What circumstance would those be?' Jude asked.

Nolan nodded again. 'You two boys are what I would call adroit. You know that word?'

'I think we can figure it out,' Josh said. 'Whatever it is, I think we've got plenty of it.'

Nolan grinned again. 'Like I said, if we meet bad guys, we treat them as they deserve. And if we meet good guys, who have fallen off the trail so to speak, we help them get on their feet again.'

'Sounds like you're a bunch of heavenly saints,' Josh said.

Nolan's grin widened. 'I wouldn't put it quite like that,' he chuckled. 'We have our high points and our low points but we struggle along in the best way we can.'

'Well, that's good,' Josh said, 'because I don't think I could live in heaven too long. The air up there might be a little rarefied for me, like trying to find your footing in the clouds.'

Nolan laughed. 'That's good, Mr Appleseed. That's really good.' He paused and looked at them each in turn. 'As it happens I'm riding out on an investigation this very day. So why don't you ride along with me?'

'You mean like you want us to ride with you?' Jude said.

'Just the two of us?' Josh added.

Nolan shrugged. 'I have a few debts to call in. Nothing too serious. Look upon it as a kind of apprenticeship or test. You just have to ride with me into town. Nothing to it really.'

There was another pause as Jude and Josh glanced at one another.

'That's fine by me, Mr Nolan,' Jude said.

'I think I can manage that, Mr Nolan,' Josh concurred.

'Good, then that's agreed.' Nolan studied them closely. 'And don't forget to bring along your shooters. As you know this is a wild country and you never know who or what you're likely to meet out there.'

'Like bears or coyotes,' Josh suggested.

Jude and Josh walked back to their hell hole of a cabin to pick up their things.

'Are you sure we're doing the right thing, Mr Appleseed?' Jude asked Josh.

Josh was strapping on his gunbelt. 'I'm not sure about anything, Mr James. In fact I never have been. I take one day at a time and hope for the right outcome. What about you?'

Jude squeezed his face up as he tried to figure things out. 'I've been thinking about this guy Brod Nolan,' he said. 'He's like a pool you come across in the middle of a forest. Everything looks calm enough on the surface, but underneath there are hidden monsters waiting to suck you down.'

'You have a good way of putting things, Mr James,' Josh said. 'And I admire that in a man.'

'Well, you have quite a good tongue on yourself as well,' Jude said. 'Maybe we should start a mutual admiration club.'

As they went out to the barn to saddle their mounts they saw Oliphant lurking by the main cabin, but as soon as he saw them he disappeared like a ghost.

'You see that?' Josh said to Jude. 'Long Hair did a disappearing act.'

'Yes, but not before I got a good peek at his ugly face,' Jude replied.

'And I saw that too. Just like His Majesty the Devil himself in a particularly ugly mood like he had a painful abscess on his butt.'

'Pride comes before a shooting,' Jude said. 'And we are the painful abscess. So what d'you figure we should do?'

'Pride comes before a fall too. You think we should shoot him before he takes a shot at us?' Josh speculated.

Jude shrugged. 'I heard some guy said, "Readiness is all". I don't know who said it but I guess he was right. So we should keep ourselves tooled up all the time just in case.'

They rode out with Nolan shortly after, headed towards the neighbouring town. Nolan rode his horse like a leisurely gent surveying his estate. He wore a tall black hat and had two guns on his hips.

'Where are the other men?' Jude asked Nolan. 'Why aren't they in on this mission?'

'You don't need to fret yourself about them,' Nolan said. 'They're resting up so they're ready for the next big enterprise.'

'And what's the next big enterprise, Mr Nolan?' Josh asked.

Nolan grinned under his wide hat. 'You sure know the right questions to ask,' he said. 'But don't push too hard. Learn to be patient and you'll soon find out.'

That was something of a short lecture, Jude thought to himself. Rather like a teacher who didn't know the answer, or didn't want to divulge it to the class.

They rode along through the high country until they came to a well-marked trail.

'This is where the stage runs,' Nolan said. 'And sometimes it carries rich pickings in the form of citizens loaded with gold.'

'You mean the rich actually ride on the stage?' Josh asked in surprise.

'Some do and some don't. But we won't concern ourselves with them right now. We have other things to think about.'

What other things? Jude wondered. He glanced at Josh and saw that he was thinking on the same question.

They came to the town after about an hour. It was quite busy with folk hurrying to and fro on their business and somewhat larger than Jude had expected. They passed saloons and eating-houses and banks, and even a few stores selling items of clothing. Occasionally people looked up as they passed and some even raised their hats to Nolan as though they knew him. Presently they came to a small store that seemed to sell everything from brushes and pots and pans to men and women's clothing.

'OK,' Nolan said. 'Tie your horses to the hitching rail and follow me.'

Jude and Josh dismounted and followed Nolan into the store. Behind the counter amidst a whole load of items stood a stout guy with a striped apron across his paunch. He had cherubic ruddy cheeks like a gnome and a grey bushy beard. He was beaming away to himself as if the world owed him a living. But Jude noticed a momentary cloud pass over his face when he recognized Nolan.

'Ah, Mr Nolan, good day to you, sir,' he crowed. 'How nice to see you, sir.'

'Good to see you too, Mr Gullivant.'

The stout man ran his eyes over Jude and Josh and, no doubt, noted the guns on their hips. 'See you brought your friends with you,' he said.

'Business associates,' Nolan corrected. 'Thought we'd just drop in to see how you're doing.'

'I'm sure you're welcome, gentlemen,' Gullivant said.

Josh nodded to him and smiled his big open smile. 'Good morrow, sir.'

Jude's smile was slightly more tight-lipped; he nodded and said nothing.

Gullivant smiled and suddenly seemed to come to life. He started wriggling his pudgy fingers. 'Now, gentlemen, why don't you come through and I'll ask my good woman to bring you refreshments, a cup of coffee, maybe, or even a bite to eat?'

Nolan nodded and grinned. 'Can't stay too long, Mr Gullivant. Things to do, you know. But I guess we could drink a glass of cold beer if you have one available.'

Gullivant dithered behind the counter. 'Of course, of course. Why don't you just step through, gentlemen, and sit yourselves down.'

Nolan led the way through to the back room like a land-lord inspecting the property. He sat down on a soft seat and waved his hand. 'Sit down, boys. Make yourselves good and comfortable.'

Jude and Josh sat down on similar soft seats as a woman as stout as Gullivant came in with drinks on a tray. 'Good day, Mr Nolan,' she greeted in a cheery manner, though Jude felt a distinct chill in the air.

'Perhaps you'd go through and attend to the customers, Mabel?' Gullivant said.

'Why, of course, dear,' she said, hurrying into the shop from where they heard the babble of voices.

Nolan raised his glass and said, 'Cheers, Mr Gullivant.'

'Cheers!' Gullivant echoed, though he wasn't drinking.

'You seem to be doing well, Mr Gullivant,' Nolan said. 'Now there's just the little matter of the money you owe me.'

Gullivant raised his eyebrows in astonishment. 'Do I still owe you money, Mr Nolan?'

'Only a matter of a few hundred dollars, Mr Gullivant.'

'Why, of course. I'm afraid it slipped my memory. How much would that be exactly?'

Nolan mentioned a figure that seemed extortionate to Jude, and Josh looked at him sideways with a kind of quizzical stare.

Gullivant took a deep breath and glanced at Jude and Josh as though making a difficult calculation. Then he said, 'Why, of course, of course.' He sprang up with surprising alacrity considering his weight, and disappeared into the shop with some speed.

Nolan looked at the Jude and Josh. 'Just a little matter of business, gentlemen,' he explained. 'But my clients can be a little reluctant at times. That's why I need men like you to support me.'

'With guns,' Josh added.

'That certainly sharpens the mind,' Nolan agreed, with a chuckle.

Gullivant hurried back into the room with a wad of notes in his hand. 'Here we are, Mr Nolan. It's exactly right. I just counted it out myself.'

'Thank you, Mr Gullivant,' Nolan said, taking the money and tucking into his pocket. 'Thanks for the drinks. Me and the boys will be on our way.' He got up and made for the door, where he turned slowly. 'See you next quarter, Mr Gullivant.'

Jude nodded to the stout man and Josh gave him an encouraging smile.

They passed through the store where everyone stopped talking and gave them an inquisitive stare. Mrs Gullivant was sitting on a stool behind the counter trying to look invisible.

Out on the sidewalk, Nolan looked up at the sun with obvious satisfaction and smiled. 'You did a real good job there, boys,' he said.

'I don't remember doing anything at all, other than looking pretty and drinking a glass of cold beer,' Josh said.

'That's what you're here for, Mr Appleseed. I collect the money and you just drink cold beer and look as pretty as you can. But not too pretty in case the clients get the wrong idea.'

Jude was about to ask about the money when he looked to his right and saw riders coming into town. He also noticed that there was a sudden thinning out of the local population as though a hailstorm was about to break over the town and they didn't want to get hit.

'Well now,' Nolan said. 'What have we here?'

'Indeed, what have we here?' Josh said, following Nolan's line of sight.

'What we have here is the Sullivan boys,' Nolan said. 'Get ready with your shooters, boys, because I think you're gonna need them.'

Jude looked at the Sullivan boys and saw that there were at least seven of them. 'That's quite a big family of Sullivans,' he said.

'Ugly too,' Josh added.

'More ugly than you can possibly believe,' Nolan said. 'Those boys would sell their mother down the river for less than a dollar. That's the way they are.'

Jude looked across the wide, dusty main street as the Sullivan boys rode up to the saloon opposite. But instead of dismounting they just sat their horses and looked to right and left as though trying to locate a guest they were supposed to meet.

'Well, that's seven against three,' Nolan said. 'I think I miscalculated. We should have brought along a few more of the boys with us.'

'Maybe we should step back inside the store and wait for them to pass along,' Josh suggested.

'Something tells me that wouldn't help a lot, especially as Dean Sullivan has seen me already.'

Jude looked across the street and saw what must be Dean Sullivan sneering in Nolan's direction. 'I think we got ourselves into some difficulty here, Mr Appleseed,' he said to Josh.

'I think you could be right, Mr James. How d'you think we should play this?'

'I think we need to defend ourselves. I just hope your shooting is as good as your punching, otherwise, we should start saying our prayers with earnest attention to detail.'

Jude was watching the Sullivan boys who were now talking among themselves and looking in their direction in a somewhat hostile manner.

'What's the plan, Mr Nolan?' Jude asked.

'The plan is to shoot straight and fast,' Nolan replied. 'Those Sullivans don't take prisoners and they're as mean as a cartload of scorpions.'

What the hell have we got ourselves into here? Jude wondered.

Dean Sullivan turned his horse and started across main street followed by two of his henchmen. The others fanned out on either side so that they could come in at angle.

Nolan drew both his guns and stepped to one side so that he wasn't framed in the doorway. 'Get yourselves some sort of cover,' he advised Jude and Josh.

Jude moved to the left where there was a convenient barrel under the ramada and Josh moved to the right behind a post which might provide some cover, but not much.

'So you decided to ride into town after all, Nolan,' Dean Sullivan shouted across the intervening space.

'Well, as you see, I'm here, Sullivan, minding my own business.'

'In that case why are you toting those two shooters in your hands?'

'That's because I've only got two hands,' Nolan shouted back. 'If I had four I'd be toting four shooters.'

Sullivan sneered. 'The way you shoot you'd be better off with six.'

'Well, I've been practising so I can shoot down skunks if I happen to come across one or two. Skunks have an awful bad smell as you are probably aware.'

Sullivan wrinkled his nose. 'You're damn right they do. I can smell that stink from here. Why don't you just step out into the street like an honest man so I can see you better?'

Nolan chuckled. 'Why don't you get off your horse and come a little closer so I've got a better target?'

Sullivan jigged his mount to one side but didn't come closer.

Jude studied the line of Sullivan's henchmen and saw they had their hands on their guns. He knew that once he had drawn his own gun he would be committed. On the other hand if the Sullivans drew theirs and started shooting he might be dead before he could make a move. His heart was pounding like a sledgehammer and he wondered if he could aim straight. He took a quick glance beyond Nolan to see what Josh might be thinking and saw Josh half crouching ready for action. Jude grasped the butt of his Colt Peacemaker and eased it in its holster. He knew it would slide out as smooth as a rattlesnake. He thought of his pa and wondered in a split second what he had used the pistol for. He felt a tension so tightly strung he could hear it singing in the air.

Something had to give and that something came when one of Sullivan's henchmen got over-nervous and drew his weapon. Nolan fired immediately and then dropped down on to one knee, blazing away with both guns.

Jude drew his Peacemaker and aimed at Dean Sullivan but before he could squeeze the trigger, Sullivan had disappeared behind his horse. Then a bullet whined past Jude so close he could almost feel it take his Stetson off his head. Suddenly his head cleared and his body was pumping adrenaline. He moved forward and started firing wildly. But at nothing. The street was filled with dust and gunsmoke and the noise of firing but there were no targets. The Sullivans had whirled away in a cloud and vanished!

Jude looked towards Nolan and Josh and saw that they were still standing. Josh was yelling a kind of war cry that might have been ancestral, and Nolan was holstering one of his guns. Out in the middle of main street lay a dead horse and dead man!

CHAPTER FIVE

Nolan stepped forward with a gun in his right hand. He looked round cautiously and held up his hand. 'OK, boys. I think they've thought better of it. So you can step out of cover. But be cautious: those Sullivan boys might come back again. Dean Sullivan won't like what happened one little bit.'

Jude went over to Josh and took him by the arm. 'Are you OK, brother?'

Josh was smiling in his usual way, but Jude felt his body shivering as though a sudden draught of wind had caught him. 'I think I just killed a man,' Josh said.

'And I think I just killed a horse,' Jude said.

They went over to inspect the two corpses and found that the horse was, in fact, still alive. Nolan went over to it and levelled his gun. 'I can't bear to see a creature suffer,' he said. The stricken horse raised its head and looked at Nolan as though begging for mercy and Nolan shot it between the eyes. Its head jerked back and fell lifeless on the ground. 'There, you're in horse heaven now,' Nolan said.

Jude felt like vomiting.

People were out the street again and a small crowd had gathered round the dead man who lay face up on the ground with eyes wide open and blood spilling. He had taken a bullet right in the middle of the forehead and was dead before he hit the ground.

'Never knew what struck him,' Nolan said. 'That must be about the best way to go.'

'Well, he won't come back to tell us, that's for sure,' Josh said. 'I wonder if he'll ever know he once lived.'

'Not on this side of eternity,' Nolan speculated.

'You could be right at that,' Josh agreed.

'You want to come over to my office?' a voice asked.

Jude saw a man looking directly at Nolan. He was short but stocky and he had a badge of office fastened to his vest.

'Good day to you, Sheriff,' Nolan said. 'Did you see what happened? Those Sullivan boys rode in and tried to shoot us down.'

The sheriff nodded grimly. 'I did see some of it, but I was busy in my office when the shooting started.'

'It was self-defence,' Nolan asserted. 'It was this *hombre* here who fired the first shot.' He pointed down at the dead man. 'Should have saved his bullet or turned it on his own head for all the good it did him.'

'Yes, well that's as maybe,' the sheriff said grimly. 'If you'll be kind enough to step into my office and give me a statement, I'd be obliged.'

The sheriff's office was sparsely furnished and businesslike and the sheriff himself couldn't have looked more ordinary unless you focused on his badge. He was stocky and barrel-chested but he looked strangely weary as though he'd seen much of the world and didn't care for it one little bit.

'Well now, Mr Nolan, what's all this about?' he enquired.

Nolan shrugged. 'Well, Sheriff, there isn't much to tell. We'd just been into the store across the way to collect a few dollars Mr Gullivant owed me and when we came out those Sullivan boys rode right up and opened fire on us. So we had to shoot back. It was a matter of shoot or be shot.'

The sheriff stifled a yawn. 'What about witnesses, Mr Nolan? Did anyone see what happened?'

'I'm not sure about that, Sheriff. You see when those scum hit us everyone disappeared from the scene.'

'That is so,' the sheriff agreed.

'Then everyone crawled out again to stare at the dead man and the dead horse,' Josh explained.

The sheriff eyed Josh suspiciously. 'Are you from down south?' he asked.

Josh smiled. 'If you mean was I a slave, the answer is yes, that was until Mr Abraham Lincoln set me free.'

The sheriff didn't look particularly impressed. He turned to Nolan again. 'This is a peaceable town, Mr Nolan, and we aim to keep it that way.'

'Tell that to Dean Sullivan, Sheriff. I just go about my rightful business, that's all.'

The sheriff sighed. 'We have a dead man out there. Someone has to pay the funeral expenses.'

'Well, that's down to the Sullivans, I guess,' Nolan replied.

Jude looked out and saw that already the funeral director and his assistant were loading the body into a pine coffin. The dead man looked like a dummy dressed as a man. The dead horse was still lying on Main Street, though a crowd was stripping off its accoutrements ready to drag it away, probably to the butchery where it would provide food for hungry townsfolk.

The sheriff got up from behind his desk. He had on a gunbelt with an ancient Colt Navy cap and ball in the holster. He peered out at the men clearing the street and sighed again. 'I have to tell you something,' he said to Nolan.

'What's that, Sheriff?'

'I'd prefer not to see you here in town again.'

Nolan nodded. 'Why's that, Sheriff?'

'That's because those Sullivans will be back just like horse flies are attracted to horse shit. And they'll want your blood, Mr Nolan.'

Jude saw Nolan's jaw muscles tighten. 'Well, that's not the best way of saying it, Sheriff, but I do agree they'll want revenge. On the other hand, I have my rights and if people owe me money I must feel free to ride in and collect my debts.' He got up from his seat and took his hat. 'I bid you good day, Sheriff, and keep the peace if you can.'

When they were on their horses again, Nolan let rip. 'Like I said, the law around here is just like a man of straw. That's why we have to make our own law.'

'You mean Nolan's Law,' Josh said, with more than a tinge of irony.

Nolan spurred his horse and rode on between the houses, some of which were clapboard while a few actually had brick façades. As they passed, faces peered out at them from stores and eating-houses and a few townsfolk turned towards them and tipped their hats.

'Are you boys feeling hungry?' Nolan asked.

Josh looked at Jude and Jude nodded.

'Shooting has sure given me an appetite,' Josh said, 'I must confess that my belly heaved when the gunplay started, but now I'm recovering it's asking me if someone cut my throat.'

'Well then it's lucky I brought supplies,' Nolan said. 'Nothing too fancy but enough to convince your belly that your throat is still in one piece. We could stop by a small eating-place I know on the edge of town but I think that might be tempting fate a little and I'm not convinced the Sullivans won't circle round and come back to haunt us. That Dean Sullivan has an powerful thirst for revenge and when his pride is involved he won't rest until he's drunk his fill.' He looked towards Jude and Josh. 'By the way, I want to thank you two boys. You earned you keep and passed the test.'

'What test would that be, Mr Nolan?' Josh asked innocently.

'I mean your apprenticeship. You did a mighty fine job there, Mr Appleseed. You too, Mr James. I'm glad to have you on board my ship, so to speak.'

'You mean shooting a man and a horse in the middle of town?' Josh said.

'Well,' Nolan said with a grin, 'I didn't mean it to be like that, but you did your job and proved yourselves and you deserve your pay. So, when we get back to the ranch, I'll peel off a few dollars and hand them over to you.'

'Thanks a lot,' Josh said.

Jude said nothing as usual. He liked to bide his time and reserve judgement until he felt certain he was justified. He still felt squeamish about that poor dead horse that had raised its head as though begging for mercy before Nolan shot it dead. And he couldn't clear his head of the picture of that dead man staring up in disbelief as he died.

As they rode on, Nolan became quite animated. In fact he started singing somewhat untunefully to himself. 'Along here we'll get off the trail a piece and eat in the shade. In the meantime maybe you'd care to take a drink out of my canteen.' He passed the canteen to Jude who took a sniff at the contents. 'Why that's rye whiskey unless I'm mistaken.'

'Just take one sip unless you want to fall out of the saddle,' Nolan advised. 'That's a mighty strong brew and we need to keep our minds sharp and ready just in case. . . .'

The sip turned into a gulp and Jude felt it coursing down his throat and into his veins like molten lava. 'Wow!' he said passing the canteen to Josh.

'Is this the devil's brew?' Josh asked, shaking his head.

'Well, if it is,' Jude said, 'that critter has a lot going for him. No wonder he has horns sprouting from his head.'

'And a face as red as the setting sun,' Josh added.

Nolan raised his hand. 'Quiet, boys, quiet!'

Jude and Josh stopped talking. The horses tossed their heads and snorted.

'You hear that?' Nolan asked.

'I hear horses galloping unless I'm mistaken,' Josh said, 'and they sound like they're in something of a hurry.'

'Get off the trail, boys, that's the Sullivans.' Nolan spurred his horse away towards a stand of trees close to the trail. Jude and Josh followed without argument and it wasn't a moment too soon. As they dismounted and crouched down in the thicket, the riders they had expected came into view and there were six of them.

'That's the Sullivans,' Nolan breathed. 'Like I suspected they're on our tail.'

'Well, they don't have much grey matter between their ears,' Josh said, 'or they haven't figured out how to use it yet because they're stirring up a lot of noise and keeping to the main trail.'

There was no time to contradict Josh's view since the Sullivans were now not much more than a gunshot away on the trail.

'What do we do now?' Jude asked quietly.

'We wait and see what happens,' Nolan said as he drew his Winchester from its sheath. 'Don't get trigger happy,' he said, 'and don't shoot unless I say so.'

They looked out between the branches as Sullivan threw up his arm and brought his small cavalcade to a halt.

He might not have much brain matter, Jude thought, but

he has a whole lot of horse sense and he knows we're somewhere around here.

Then Dean Sullivan peered towards them and dismounted. 'Those skunks are in that stand of trees over there,' he said, clearly enough for his henchmen to hear as well as everyone else for a half a mile around.

'What do we do?' one of Sullivan's riders asked.

'We flush them out and kill them like the rats they are,' Sullivan said, drawing his carbine and looking towards the stand of trees.

Jude pointed his Peacemaker at one of the Sullivan gang and waited. This is no place for a man of peace like me, he thought.

'You ready, man?' Josh asked from close beside him.

'Just about as ready as I can be,' Jude said. The thought of having to kill a man got right into the marrow of his bones like frost in deep winter.

Nolan levered his Winchester and peered out between the trees towards the Sullivan bunch. 'Stop being a damn fool, Sullivan,' he shouted. 'Nobody needs to get killed here.'

'It's too late for that,' Sullivan's voice came back from behind his horse. 'You already killed one of my men, and blood calls for blood. That's the law.'

'That's the law of the jungle, man,' Josh responded.

'You should know all about that,' Sullivan came back. 'Why don't you just shut your mouth while you've still got a mouth to shut?'

Jude looked at Josh and said, 'Don't let yourself get riled up, Mr Appleseed.'

But it was too late. Josh rose up with his Winchester and took a bead on Dean Sullivan's horse. 'Why do you hide behind an innocent horse?' he shouted. 'Haven't you got the guts to come out and face me man to man? Then you'll see what a man can do!'

As if it understood, Sullivan's horse suddenly jigged to one side to reveal Sullivan crouching with his carbine levelled at Josh. But before he could fire, Nolan pushed his Winchester between the branches and fired a shot. It went wide of Sullivan but it had an explosive effect on Sullivan's men. The five suddenly pulled away from the trail and started to disperse in all directions, firing their guns as they went.

At that moment Jude saw Dean Sullivan fall down on one knee and discharge his weapon. Josh jerked back and fell without a word.

'That bastard killed him!' Jude roared. He ran to the edge of the thicket and fired his weapon towards Dean Sullivan.

'Keep down!' he heard Nolan shouting, as he ran on towards Dean Sullivan.

Sullivan fired a shot in Jude's direction the moment before he fell and the bullet missed Jude by no more than a holy inch. Jude levered himself up on his elbow and reached for his Winchester, just as a man came riding towards him. It was one of Sullivan's henchmen who was leaning forward to gun down on him. There was little Jude could do to avoid the rider's gun, but he tried to roll away and protect himself. As he did so, the thought flashed through his racing brain: I'm going to die! This is the end! He didn't hear the explosion or see the flash. The man's horse veered to one side and the man who was intent on killing him suddenly jerked in the saddle and fell towards him.

Jude lay gasping on the earth for a moment, wondering where he had been hit and why he felt no pain. Guns were firing all round him and men were yelling and cursing, but all he could see was the man shuddering and dying beside him.

'Water,' the man gasped. 'Give me water for God's sake!' Then he shuddered and his eyes glazed over in death.

*

The next thing Jude knew Nolan was bending over him and raising his head. 'Have you been hit?' Nolan asked.

'I'm not sure,' Jude said. 'I can't feel anything.'

'Take a shot of this.' Nolan pressed the canteen to his lips and he took a good long pull at the rye whiskey. He felt it going right down to his toes like a raging fire but it jerked him back to the land of the living. 'What happened?' he asked.

'They pulled out,' Nolan told him. 'I think I winged one of them.'

'They got my buddy,' Jude said. 'Did Sullivan kill him?' He struggled to his feet and staggered back towards the stand of trees. Josh was lying on his back with blood oozing from his chest and his eyes were closed, but he was gritting his teeth and groaning. Jude knelt down beside him and inspected a wound that was high in his chest just below the collar bone.

'Lie still while I look at that wound!' Nolan commanded.

Josh's eyes rolled round to look at Nolan and he grimaced with pain. 'I don't think I passed the test, after all,' he groaned.

'Well, I've got news for you, Mr Appleseed. I believe you're going to pull through.'

Despite his groaning, Josh actually managed to grin.

Nolan went to his horse and reached into his saddle-bag for something. 'First thing we do is we stop the bleeding,' he said. 'Now, Mr James, I want you to press this against the wound just hard enough to staunch the bleeding. D'you think you can do that?'

'Sure I can do it,' Jude said. He took the pad and pressed it where the blood was flowing. Josh gave a piercing cry and kicked out against the pain. Then he shuddered and passed out.

70

'He fainted away,' Nolan said, 'but he'll come round soon enough as long as we can staunch the flow of blood.'

'Then what do we do?' Jude asked.

'Well, we can't get him to the ranch. It's too far and he might die on the way. Our only chance is to get him to the sawbones in town.'

'That won't be easy,' Jude said. 'Maybe if I rode back to find the doc, he might come back with me.'

Nolan stood up and peered around as though he was looking for possibilities or maybe just wondering if those Sullivans were still somewhere in the vicinity.

Then the Angel of Mercy appeared. It didn't have glittering wings or shining armour; it came in the form of a stagecoach drawn by four brown horses heading towards town.

'Wait here,' Nolan said, somewhat needlessly since Josh was still out cold. He walked towards the trail and waved his Winchester in the air.

The stagecoach driver drew his team to a halt and the man riding shotgun fingered his weapon apprehensively.

'Howdy, Mr Nolan,' the driver said. 'This wouldn't be a hold-up, would it?'

'Not today, Mr Tandy,' Nolan shouted back. 'We have a little problem here and we just wondered if you could give a little help.'

The driver looked about him. 'I see you have a dead man lying there.'

'Yep,' Nolan replied, 'and we have a badly wounded man too in grave need of attention from Doc Winter, the sawbones in town. If we try to lift our man into the saddle he might die on us. Is there any chance you might take him on board and carry him into town? He's bleeding bad.'

The stage driver looked down at Josh with a critical eye. 'Is that a man of colour I can see?'

'That's Josh Appleseed,' Jude said, 'and he's my partner.'

The driver looked as though he was about to say something, but before he could open his mouth again a face looked out from the stagecoach door. 'Is this a hold-up?' a man said.

'No, sir,' Nolan replied. 'This is an errand of mercy. We've got a wounded man here and we need to get into town urgently.'

'Well in that case,' the man said, 'why don't you just get him into the coach, so we can drive on immediately. We have room; he can lie on the seat.'

Jude now saw several other faces peering out of the coach window but some weren't quite so welcoming.

The driver said, 'I'm not sure about that. We don't want blood in the coach. It's sort of unhygienic.'

'If it's a matter of hygiene or death I'm willing to give up my place for the wounded man.' The man clambered down from the coach. 'Here, let me help you lift him in. If necessary I can borrow his horse and ride alongside the coach.'

Josh had now regained consciousness though he looked somewhat dazed. They raised him to his feet and, with a good deal of help, he limped towards the coach. He managed to drag himself up the step and into the coach where he lay down with a deep sigh of relief.

'Now drive on slowly,' the man who had given up his place said to the driver.

The Good Samaritan then mounted Josh's horse and they rode on towards town. The man turned to Jude. 'So you're the wounded man's *amigo*?' he said.

'He's my buddy. We ride together,' Jude agreed.

'I'm the Reverend Jeremy Justice.' The man stuck out a

friendly hand. 'I'm sort of a wandering preacher trying to bring peace and harmony to this wild land. Most people call me Jerry the Preacher, or in some cases the Reverend Jerry. I'm hoping to abide in the town nearby for a while.'

Jude took the proffered hand. 'Pleased to meet you, Reverend Jerry.'

'So there's been a shooting here?' the reverend said.

Jude explained that Mr Nolan had been in town collecting debts when the Sullivans came down like the hosts of Ninevah.

The Reverend Jerry nodded but didn't smile, though Jude noticed he had crow's feet at the corners of his eyes and deep creases at the side of his lips which did indicate a smiling nature. 'Have you two boys been with Mr Nolan long?' the reverend asked.

'No more than a few days,' Jude affirmed, 'though it seems much longer.'

'Well, you take care,' the Reverend Jerry advised. 'I hope your good friend survives.'

The stagecoach driver had been in the job for several years and he prided himself on his good judgement. So he drove into town quite slowly and steadily to keep the patient alive. He drew the coach to a halt right outside Doc Winter's office which also served as the town hospital. It was quite small and there was room for maybe half-a-dozen patients. Nolan, Jude, and the Reverend Jerry dismounted and the priest strode ahead.

Doc Winters was in the middle of bandaging a patient who had caught his hand on a exposed nail. The doc looked up in alarm. 'I didn't hear you knock.' His eyes lit up and he smiled. 'Why, hello Mr Nolan and Reverend Jerry. What can I do for you?'

'We've got a badly wounded man out here in the stage,'

Nolan explained, 'and he needs urgent attention.'

The doctor snipped the bandage with his scissors. 'I think that'll be all right now, Mr Pinkney,' he said. 'Lead the way, gentlemen.'

They went out to the stagecoach where the passengers were disembarking, one or two muttering angrily to themselves.

'The wounded man is lying on the seat in the coach,' the driver explained needlessly.

'I'd best have a looksee,' the doctor said. And he sprang with surprising agility into the coach.

After a few moments he climbed down again. 'We must get him inside,' he said, 'but we must avoid further injury. So, keep his right arm steady.'

Before anyone else could move, Jude leaped into the coach. Josh was already sitting up, ready to disembark. Jude helped him onto his feet, making sure to avoid touching his right arm or shoulder. Josh looked down. 'It's a long ways down there,' he muttered through gritted teeth. He reached down for Nolan and the Reverend Jerry who were both trying to assist him.

'Slide yourself down on your left side while I steady your leg,' the doctor said. Josh gritted his teeth and stepped down cautiously. Then they helped him into the doctor's office.

CHAPTER SIX

Doc Winter carried out a thorough examination and made his diagnosis. 'No bones broken but I guess the bullet is still lodged high in the chest. So the first thing we have to do is dig it out.'

Josh was lying on a bed gritting his teeth. 'Can you do that?' he asked the doctor.

'Oh, I can do it, sure enough,' Dr Winter said. 'Done a plenty of them in my time. In the war I was an army surgeon and I had to chop off any number of legs and arms, let alone digging for bullets.' He smiled at the patient. 'Don't you worry yourself, Mr Appleseed, I'll have that bullet out in less than a tick tock. But first I must give you a little whiff of something to make you forget the world for a while.'

'You gonna kill me?' Josh asked him.

The doctor smiled. 'I don't think it will come to that, but if I don't get that bullet out it might indeed lead to your demise.'

Josh looked none too confident but he resigned himself to his fate. 'So when can I go to whatever I might call home?'

'Well, you'll have to bide here for a time, maybe as long as a week or two,' the doctor advised. 'That shouldn't be too hard to bear.' He looked at Nolan.

Nolan nodded. 'Just as long as it takes,' he said.

Jude didn't like Nolan too much but he was beginning to see his human side. Ever since they rode into town and encountered the Sullivan bunch he had been asking himself what the hell he and Josh had got themselves into. 'Am I now nothing but a hired gunman?' he asked himself.

After the doc had put Josh to sleep, he said, 'I think you boys had best step outside for a while. This might not be pretty and I don't want to upset your breakfast. I need to work fast right now.'

Jude and Nolan went out and sat on the bench under the ramada. The stage had now pulled away but the Reverend Jerry was still hovering around like a big black benevolent crow looking for somewhere to perch.

'Well,' he said to Nolan, 'what do you intend to do, sir?'

Nolan looked up at the reverend sharply. 'That's for me to decide,' he said. 'I'll know just as soon as Mr Appleseed has survived his operation.' It was clear to Jude that Nolan had no love for the preacher. Indeed, they came from two different schools of thought entirely.

'Well then, I'll be moving on,' the Reverend Jerry said, raising his big black hat. He gave Jude a searching look and stepped off the sidewalk. 'See you in church, so to speak,' he added somewhat ironically.

Jude looked at Nolan and saw that he was grinning to himself. 'Those so-called holy men are all the same,' Nolan said. 'They're all full of holy shit.'

'That holy shit might have saved Josh's life,' Jude told him.

'That's true,' Nolan agreed. 'Every holy shit has at least one good deed up his sleeve. He probably thinks the Man up there is chalking it up in his favour. Why don't you have a cigar? Help you to relax a little.' He held out a case with a cigar protruding from it.

'Like I told you, thanks for the offer, but I don't smoke,' Jude said. 'I seen men coughing their hearts out after smoking for a year or so.'

'Well, please yourself, boy. You change your mind there'll always be one at hand for you to enjoy.'

Jude looked up and saw the stumpy figure of the sheriff stepping towards them across Main Street. He still seemed kind of world weary. As he drew close, he looked down at Nolan and sighed. 'I hear one of your boys got himself shot up,' he said.

'Evening, Sheriff,' Nolan greeted. 'Took one in the chest. The doc's digging out the bullet right now as we speak. He was shot down by one of the Sullivan boys, but we think he's gonna survive.'

'What do you aim to do?' the sheriff asked.

'I'm thinking on it, Sheriff, I'm thinking on it,' Nolan replied.

'Well, don't take too long thinking, Mr Nolan, because it's almost sundown.'

Nolan lit a cigar and inhaled deeply. 'I'll let you know when I've come to a conclusion, Sheriff.'

'I'm glad to hear that, Mr Nolan,' the sheriff said, 'because as long as you're in town the air seems kind of polluted.'

Jude saw the muscles in Nolan's jaw flex. 'Well, maybe you should look behind you and sniff your own pile of shit,' he said.

The sheriff stared at Nolan for a moment and then glanced at Jude. He raised one eyelid, and then turned and walked away.

Nolan glanced at Jude and laughed, not the pleasantest of laughs; it was the sort that chilled your bones but you weren't quite sure why. 'He's just about as useful as that pile of shit I just mentioned.' Nolan inhaled deeply again. 'What we do now, Mr James, is we ride down Main Street and call in a favour.'

'In what form would that be, Mr Nolan?' Jude enquired.

'That would be we stay the night in the best hotel in town,' Nolan replied. 'We take the best dinner in town and then put aside our worries until the morning. After a good breakfast we can think on the future.'

They walked into the hospital again to enquire after the patient. Doctor Winter came to meet them.

'The patient's sleeping like a baby now,' the doc said. He held up a bullet by his forceps. 'I got this bitch of a bullet out,' he said. 'Now all we have to do is to wait on the healing process. If you gentlemen will come back tomorrow morning, we'll see how Mr Appleseed is doing. It wasn't nearly as bad as I had feared.'

'That will be just fine, Dr Winter,' Nolan said.

They mounted their horses and rode on until they came to The Grand Hotel, which was reputed to be the best hotel in town.

'Here, take my horse, Mr James. I'll just go in and check,' Nolan said. He looked left and right down Main Street and then dismounted.

Jude sat his horse and waited. He had a feeling of deep unease as though he was being watched from every window and doorway. Once again he wondered what he had got himself into. The town was alive with half-muted sounds – people shouting and discordant music leaking from the various saloons abutting Main Street. Yet the air was heavy with menace.

After no more than a minute or two, a man emerged from the entrance to the hotel and bowed in his direction. He looked like some kind of old English butler. 'Please come right inside, Mr James,' he said genially. 'I'll have your horses taken to the stables.' Jude dismounted and handed over the reins to a youngish man who looked only too pleased to accept them.

The 'butler' then ushered him into the Grand Hotel. He found Nolan already ensconced behind a table with a tumbler of whiskey in his hand and a Havana cigar in his mouth. Nolan gestured towards a seat. 'Sit yourself down, my friend,' he said expansively. 'They tell me dinner will be served in ten minutes. How d'you like your steak?'

'Just as it comes,' Jude said. He sat down next to Nolan who was sitting with his back to the wall. 'I always sit with my back to the wall,' he explained. 'Many an overconfident *hombre* sat with his back to the door. Did you ever hear of James Butler Hickok?'

'I can't say I ever have,' Jude said.

'Hickok was a sheriff and he made a lot of enemies. Thought he was bullet proof but somebody shot him in the back of the head, which confounded his opinion somewhat, but I don't suppose he worried too much about it because he fell stone dead with the cards in his hand. They say pride comes before a fall, I believe, and that puffed up sheriff sure was proud.' He gave that rather harsh unfriendly laugh again.

Jude looked up and saw the 'butler' coming towards them accompanied by a man with a trolley on which were plates of steaming food. But the person who actually placed the plates before them on the table was a young woman of colour. Jude saw an expression of terror in her eyes as though she was a slave. She glanced at him timidly as she placed his food before him on the table and he gave her a wink.

'How come?' Jude said to Nolan.

'How come what?' Nolan replied.

'Well, Mr Nolan, how come you just lift your finger and the

whole world stops to do your bidding?'

Nolan grinned. 'That's what I like about you two boys,' he said. 'You got brains between your ears and you don't give much of a damn for anybody.' He took up his cigar and inhaled deeply. Jude noticed he smoked even as he ate. He had never seen that in a man before.

'In answer to your question,' Nolan said, 'people here respect me for two reasons: the first is I have a big investment in this town.'

'What does that mean?' Jude asked him.

'It means I own most of it. I have big stakes in this particular establishment and most people in this town owe me money. That damned stupid sheriff hasn't realized it yet but his job depends on my generosity.'

'What about those Sullivans?' Jude asked. 'You don't own them, do you?'

Nolan knitted his brows momentarily. 'That Sullivan bunch are trying to move in on me. So I need to do something about that.'

'I see,' Jude said, though in fact he didn't quite see. 'So where do Josh and me fit in?'

Nolan made smoke rings in the air with his cigar. 'That depends on where you want to fit in, Mr James. I could make you richer than you ever dreamed you'd be.' He grinned and nodded. 'Why don't you just pitch into that steak and I'll order you another if you feel so inclined, And, by the way, I saw you wink at that young black woman. If you'd like her to share your bed with you tonight, you have only to say so. That can be arranged too.'

'Thank you, Mr Nolan, but I think I'll miss out on that one.'

After the meal they were shown to their rooms. Nolan's was

like the royal suite and Jude's was much more modest, though it was comfortable enough.

Before Nolan closed his door, he looked down the corridor in the direction of the stairs. 'Keep that shooter of yours handy,' he said, 'and don't forget what I told you about Hickok who might have been with us to this day if he hadn't been so cocksure of himself.' Then he disappeared into the room and Jude heard the bolt slide across.

As Jude went to his own room he heard the rustle of skirts behind him and, looking back, he saw the black girl coming towards him. He stopped and she paused, took a tremulous breath and spoke. 'Where do you want me, master?' she asked quietly.

Jude smiled. 'Why don't you just go to your bed and get yourself some sleep?' he suggested.

The girl opened her eyes wide and he saw they were bright with intelligent enquiry. 'So you don't want me?' she asked.

'What's your name?' he asked her.

She shook her head. 'What's that to you?' she asked with a hint of resentment.

'How long have you worked here?' he asked.

The girl scowled. 'Are you some kind of judge, or something?'

'I don't judge, I observe,' he said.

'What does that mean?'

'It means I use my eyes and make use of my brain,' he replied.

The girl gave him a faint smile of suspicion. 'But you carry a gun. That means you're a gunman.'

Jude grinned back at her. 'You can't always judge an animal by its skin, miss. Things aren't necessarily what they seem to be.'

The girl shrugged her shoulders and relaxed a little.

'When you closed your eye at me down there I thought it was a signal of some kind.'

'Sure it was signal,' he said. 'It meant I could see what you were thinking and I wanted you to know not to worry.'

The girl gave a brief sigh. 'The answer to your questions are: I've been here two years and my name is Sarah Jane and I'm twenty summers old.'

'Twenty summers,' he said. 'Isn't that the way the Indians talk about their ages?'

She shrugged. 'My father was Indian,' she said.

Jude looked at her and smiled. 'Well now, like I said, you go and rest, and maybe I shall see you again in the morning.'

The girl gave a slight curtsey and tiptoed off down the corridor.

Jude went into his room and locked the door. He was tired but he had a lot to think about.

He got up early. His night had been full of dreams in which the ghosts of the past seemed to rise up and haunt him: his pa and ma seemed to beckon to him but when they spoke he couldn't hear them properly or make out what they were trying to say. Nevertheless, he dashed cold water on to his face and felt ready to get on with the day. Somewhere in the back of his mind he had reached decisions but he didn't know what they were yet.

Nolan was at the table waiting for him and, as usual, he had a fat cigar in his hand.

'Ah, Mr James! Please sit down. We have a lot to talk about but first you must join me in a hearty breakfast.'

As Jude sat down at the table, the girl Sarah Jane approached with his breakfast on a tray. He looked up and caught her eye but she gave no sign.

As Nolan had promised the breakfast was indeed hearty: several eggs and an abundance of ham, and a large can of coffee too. Nolan had enjoyed the same, though with a bottle of rye whiskey on the side. He gulped down the coffee and sipped the whiskey alternately. 'I eat to keep myself alive,' he explained, 'and I live to drink,' he added. 'You only live once, Mr James, so you might as well make the best of it.' He raised his glass, 'Don't you agree, my friend?'

Jude raised his coffee mug but made no reply.

Their horses were waiting for them at the hitching-rail. Nolan mounted up and glanced down Main Street, first left and then right. 'Can't be too wary,' he said. 'You never know what or who will be coming round the next bend in the road.'

In fact, a man was riding towards them in a leisurely fashion, but it wasn't Dean Sullivan or one of his bunch; it was that black benevolent crow, Jerry the Preacher. The Reverend Jerry reined in and raised his hand in greeting. 'Why, good morning to you, gentlemen. What a fine day it is to be sure. Will you be riding my way?'

'I'm still thinking on that, Mr Jerry,' Nolan replied tersely.

'I thought so,' the Reverend Jerry said cheerily. 'I'm on my way to look in on that friend of yours to see how he's faring.'

Jude glanced back at the Grand Hotel and the 'butler' waving to them like a king acknowledging his subjects, but his attention was drawn to a window above where he saw the girl Sarah Jane looking at them between half-drawn curtains. He raised his hand in greeting and they rode on towards the hospital.

Doctor Winter was sitting at his desk when they went in.

'How's the patient?' Nolan asked loudly.

'Mr Appleseed is surprisingly sprightly for a man in his condition,' the doctor replied.

'What is his condition?' Nolan demanded.

'Is he receiving visitors?' the Reverend Jerry asked.

'You'd better come through and see for yourselves,' the

83

doctor said.

They went through and found Josh sitting in a chair with his shoulder bandaged and his arm in a sling. His eyes were shining and he was smiling. 'I'm glad you've come,' he said. 'I'm good and ready to leave.'

Doctor Winter frowned. 'I don't think that's a good idea, Mr Appleseed,' he said. 'You should stay here and rest for a week at least. I can't be accountable if you leave any sooner.'

The Reverend Jerry nodded in agreement. 'Take care, young man, take care. You've only got one life on earth, you know.'

Nolan disagreed. 'This young dude is tough,' he said. 'I think we can take care of him back at the ranch.'

Jude wasn't quite convinced, but he could see the point. With those Sullivans around anything might happen. 'You think you can manage the ride?' he asked Josh.

'I reckon I'll be as good in the saddle as I am on Mother Earth,' he said. 'If you'd be kind enough to hoist me up, I'll be just fine.'

The doctor continued to object, but Josh was insistent. In fact Josh got into the saddle with surprising agility, considering his wound, though he did groan a little.

'Thank you kindly, Doctor,' Nolan said. 'I'm much obliged for all you've done.'

The doctor grunted.

The rest of them mounted up and Nolan looked down Main Street in both directions. The Reverend Jerry was on his horse, humming away to himself quite tunefully. 'Mind if I ride along with you for a while?' he asked Nolan.

Nolan gave him a slightly suspicious glance. 'How far along?' he asked.

The Reverend Jerry smiled. 'Not far,' he said. 'I have a homesteader friend just off the trail and he needs to see me.

His wife has difficulties that I might be able to fix.'

'Is that so?' Nolan said.

They rode down Main Street and out on the trail to where they had met the stagecoach the day before. All seemed peaceful and quiet except for the birds singing in the trees.

'Don't you just love the sound of those innocent creatures?' the Reverend Jerry asked.

Nolan chuckled. 'I don't believe there's anything innocent about them,' he said. 'They're just what they are. They fight and squabble just like us.'

'I believe you're right, Mr Nolan,' the reverend replied cheerfully. 'The difference is we know what we're doing and they don't. They do what they do by instinct and we do it by design.'

Nolan gave that not altogether pleasant laugh of his. 'Well, you might be right about that, Reverend. That's your trade so you have to believe it.'

The reverend waved his hand. 'I have to branch off here,' he said. 'My friends live just off to the right a piece. So I'll bid you good day, my friends.' He took off his big black hat and held it up. 'Go in peace, my friends. Go in peace.' He turned and rode away off the trail.

'That *hombre*'s crazy as a loon,' Nolan said after the preacher had gone. 'He lives in a land of dreams.'

Jude and Josh exchanged glances and grinned.

'How you feeling?' Jude asked.

'Fair to poorly,' Josh said, 'fair to poorly.'

They stopped briefly to rest and water the horses. Josh stayed in the saddle since it was such a struggle to dismount. Then they rode on until they reached the ranch. Despite the somewhat primitive conditions Jude felt like the Prodigal Son returning home and he hoped the welcome would be as good! In fact, most of the hands were away on some mysterious mission. As they rode up Jake and his daughter appeared at the door. He was carrying a shotgun which he lowered as soon as he saw Nolan and the boys.

'Good to see you back, Mr Nolan,' he said.

'Glad to be back,' Nolan replied.

'Everything go well?'

Nolan dismounted. 'Could have been better,' he growled. 'The Sullivan bunch showed up and we had a shoot out in town. We had to kill two of those scumbags but Jude and Josh here did well.'

Nancy stared up at Josh in dismay. 'You got shot!' she cried.

'Took one high in the chest,' Josh said, 'but the doc extracted the bullet and the healing process is going along well enough.'

Nancy looked really concerned. 'You mean you rode all the way back here in that state?'

'Against doctor's orders,' Jude explained.

Jake took a hand. 'Why don't we get you down from your horse so's you can rest awhile?'

They were all eager to help, but Nancy now showed her mettle. 'Take care now," she said. 'We don't want the bleeding to start again.'

Josh cautiously swung his leg over the saddle and they helped him down. Then they went into the cabin to eat some of that fine stew Jude remembered. He wasn't quite sure what was in it but it tasted good!

'What's with that Sullivan bunch?' Jake asked Nolan.

'Well, I've been thinking on that,' Nolan replied, 'and I reckon we have no choice.'

'You talking war?' the old man said.

Nolan lit a cigar and considered matters. 'I'm not talking,' he said. 'We already have war. I'm talking tactics. We have to tread on the snake before it treads on us. Like it says in the so-called Holy Book. That's what I'm talking.'

Jude and Josh went over to their small cabin and got ready to turn in. Jude lit the oil lamp and stretched out on his cot. 'Did you hear what the man said?' he asked.

'I think I heard right,' Josh responded. 'He used the word war unless I'm slightly off my head.'

'You heard right, man,' Jude said. 'It seems there's a range war between Nolan and those Sullivan boys. Which means we're now hired guns.'

'I believe that might be true,' Josh said. 'But I'm no good with a gun in my right hand at the moment until my shoulder heals.'

'I believe Nolan is thinking long term on that,' Jude said. 'He probably thinks of you as an investment for the future.'

Josh looked thoughtful. 'Is that meant to be a compliment?' he asked.

Jude creased his brow. 'That's a fact, Mr Appleseed. We're dealing with facts here and we need to weigh up the consequences.'

'You could be right at that,' Josh said.

There was a gentle knock at the door. The two men exchanged glances. Jude took his gun and went to the door. Nancy was outside holding a bag. 'How is Mr Appleseed?' she asked.

'Please come in, Miss Nancy.'

The girl came in and looked down at Josh. 'How are you, Mr Appleseed?'

'I'm passing well,' he said. 'I'm passing well. And how are you?'

Jude saw the girl's face redden over.

She raised her bag as a kind of offering. 'I thought you might like me to check your wound, make sure it's healing properly. I've brought whiskey to pour on it to stop infection.'

Josh beamed at her. 'That's real kind of you, Miss Nancy, but I don't think we should disturb it right now. It feels just fine. But why don't you come back tomorrow to check? That might be helpful.' He opened his dark eyes wide and beamed at her again.

Nancy blushed even deeper. 'I'll do that, Mr Appleseed,' she said. She glanced at Jude and left.

Jude looked at Josh and could have sworn that he blushed too. 'That young woman has taken a real shine to you, my friend,' he said.

Josh's smile widened and he said. 'That's what comes of an ex-slave taking a bullet in the chest, Mr James.'

CHAPTER SEVEN

Josh was lying in his cot half asleep. Jude was sitting on a crate looking down at him.

'You got something on your mind, Mr James?' Josh asked.

'I've been thinking on our general position, Mr Appleseed.'

'And what are your conclusions, Mr James?'

Jude wrinkled his brow. 'I've been thinking about Fate. That's what I've been thinking about.'

Josh gave him a puzzled grin. 'That's a pretty deep subject, my friend. Are you quite sure you're sober?'

Jude shook his head. 'If you want it in broad terms, I've been thinking about our particular fate, yours and mine, that is.'

Josh pushed himself up by his left elbow. 'Please explain, my friend. I don't fully understand.'

Jude leaned forward. 'I'll do my best,' he said. 'As I see it, it's like this. You and me, we strike out West hoping to make a better life for ourselves. But so far we don't come to a land of milk and honey but we meet this guy Nolan who is about as straight as the little tight curls on your head.'

Josh grinned. 'I can't fault you on that, Mr Appleseed. You mean he's as straight as his own two front teeth.'

Jude nodded. 'And as stained too from all those cigars he smokes.'

Josh swung his legs off the cot. 'Tell me something new, Mr James. Tell me something new.'

Jude screwed up his face as though thinking didn't come easily to him. 'The first thing that comes to mind is he seems to own most of the town and yet he lives in this modest dump which is far from the comforts of the town.'

'I've been thinking on those lines, too,' Josh admitted.

'So he's rich and he lives poor,' Jude continued.

'Why do you suppose that is?' Josh asked.

'Well, I haven't quite worked that out yet. But what I have worked out is I never aimed to be a killer when I started out West.'

'I'm with you on that one too,' Josh agreed. 'And so far I've killed two men and got myself shot in the chest. In fact, I'm damn lucky to be alive and I keep thinking of that man in the Sullivan bunch I shot down, the way his eyes were staring up at the sky as though he couldn't believe in his own misfortune.'

'That's a very interesting thought,' Jude conceded.

'And another thing,' Josh said. 'I believe there's gonna be a real ruckus sooner or later and probably sooner. You remember what Nolan said about the Sullivan bunch?'

'I believe he said something about sorting them out before they sorted us out', Jude gave Josh a twisted grin. 'And I'm not sure I want to be among the sorted or among the sorters when it happens.'

They stared at one another for a full ten seconds. Then Jude said, 'Then what do we do, Mr Appleseed?'

Josh laughed. 'Well, Mr James, we have a choice. We either stay and take what comes, or we light out and hope for something better to drift our way. Except that might not be so easy.'

Jude gave him an enquiring look. 'Why should that be so, Mr Appleseed?'

'That's because I have an ingrained hatred of slavery in any form, Mr James, and I know a slave when I see one.'

'Now what does that mean, Mr Appleseed?'

Josh took a deep breath. 'You said that Nancy had taken a shine to me and I've noticed it too. That young woman is nothing but a slave here as I'm sure you've noticed.' He waited for Jude's response.

Jude gave a slight nod. 'I've noticed she's a fine-looking young lady, if that's what you mean.'

'What I mean is, if I'm to leave this ornery bunch, I can't cut out without offering that young woman the chance of freedom.'

Jude regarded him steadily for a moment. 'What are you saying?' he asked. 'This is serious talking, Mr Appleseed.'

'I believe I am serious, Mr James.'

They extinguished the lamp and lay down to sleep. Josh was still regaining his strength after the wound, so he he was soon in the depths of slumber. Jude wasn't quite as tired, so he lay back and reflected on matters, and soon the image of that young woman in Grand Hotel rose before him. Sarah Jane. He remembered their conversation on the stairs and her question, 'Where do you want me?' as though she was nothing more than a piece of merchandise, or a slave. Yes, a slave, he thought, just like Nancy!

He heard the gentle snores of his friend Josh as he drifted off to sleep.

He was dreaming of a long corridor and a young woman waving to him from a high window when he suddenly woke to the sound of cockcrow and of horses and men.

Suddenly there was a tap tap on the door and he leaped out of bed and grabbed his gun. What a way to wake up! he thought as he opened the door to see Nancy standing there and smiling.

'Good morning to you,' she said. 'I thought you should know the boys are here and they're like wolves with hunger, so I wondered if I should bring breakfast across so that Mr Appleseed can have his share before it's all gone?'

'Well, thank you for that, Miss Nancy,' Josh said from behind Jude. He was out of bed with a blanket wrapped around his middle region. 'Good morning,' he said. 'I'm grateful for your consideration but I've slept real well and I feel mighty refreshed.'

Nancy gave a slight curtsey. 'Well then,' she said, 'I'll be sure to save you something for when you come across.' She bobbed and smiled and withdrew.

Jude helped Josh into his pants. 'That young woman sure has taken a shine to you,' he laughed.

'That's because I'm the best-looking black man she ever saw,' Josh agreed.

After they'd ducked their heads under the pump they walked over to the main cabin at the entrance of which Long Hair was waiting. As they approached, he held his head on one side gave them a sardonic grin. 'I hear you took one in the shoulder,' he said to Josh without undue sympathy.

'Indeed I did,' Josh replied, 'but I'm still in the land of the living as you can see.'

Long Hair was standing right in the doorway as before.

'Maybe you could step aside to let us pass,' Jude said politely.

'Maybe I could and then maybe I couldn't!' Long Hair sneered.

'Well, then, we don't want a repeat performance, do we?' Josh said.

Long Hair looked him up and down and said, 'I don't think that's likely unless you want me to break your arm off. '

'Well now,' Jude said 'you'll have to break my arms off first, you mangy long-haired cur.'

He saw anger like lightning on a particularly dark night flash in Long Hair's eyes. The next second he saw that he was about to reach for his gun. This is now or never, he thought, but before he could slam a fist into the man's gut, a voice came from close beside him. 'OK, boys, that's enough shenanigans. We have work to do and every man is gonna count.'

Nolan stood beside them, waving his cigar.

Long Hair's sneer turned to a servile grin. 'That's OK, Mr Nolan. We were just kidding around.'

Nolan chuckled. 'Well, then, I think the kidding around has to stop because I need men around who can work together if we're going to rid ourselves of those Sullivan sons-of-bitches.'

'You don't need to worry on that, Mr Nolan,' Long Hair said, stepping to one side to let them through.

As they walked into the eating-hall they were surprised to see up to ten or twelve men eating and smoking and drinking at the tables.

'The gathering of the clans,' Jude said.

'Looks like Nolan was right,' Josh said. 'And it's gonna be all out war with those Sullivans.'

They went over to collect their food and Jake gave them a shrewd scrutinizing look. 'Good morning,' he said.

'Good morning,' Josh replied.

Jake leaned towards him and lowered his voice. 'I'd sure like a word with you, Mr Appleseed,' he half whispered. 'That's when you have the time.'

'Indeed, I'll make the time, Jake,' Josh said.

They took their chuck from Nancy and sat down at a table

close by. Josh looked across at her and smiled.

As they ate their breakfast, Jake came over and perched on the bench beside Josh, and Jude moved up a little to make sure they could speak in private.

'Well, it's like this, Mr Appleseed,' the old man said.

Josh turned to look him squarely in the face. 'No need to beat about the bush. I know full well what's on your mind. I'm black and you're white and you've come to believe all blacks are no better than slaves.'

Jake stared at him in alarm. 'That's not what I have in mind at all. In fact I would call you sort of mid-brown and when I look in the mirror I see I'm not so much white as mid grey.'

Josh looked at him for a moment and then broke into a deep guffaw of laughter. It was so loud that most of the men at the other tables stopped to look up and listen.

Jake looked even more alarmed. 'I guess I chose the wrong moment,' he said. 'I just thought—'

Josh nodded. 'I know what you thought, and I've been thinking on the same lines.' He slid closer along the bench and lowered his voice. 'The answer to the question you wanted to ask me is yes, with your permission I will, but only on one condition.'

'And what's that?' Jake asked quietly.

Josh looked at him squarely. 'The condition is that Nancy agrees to it too.'

Before they could say any more, there was a sudden hush among the men and everyone looked towards Nolan who was standing up with his back to the wall facing the door. He took the fat cigar from his mouth and rapped on the table with a glass to gain attention. Then he cleared his throat and spoke. Jude thought it was like a politician trying to rustle up votes or a preacher about to praise the Lord. But Nolan wasn't much of an orator and he certainly didn't have the gift of

94

tongues. All he had was bags of money which spoke well enough on his behalf.

'Well now, boys,' he croaked in his cigar-laden voice. 'I've got news for you. You've ridden a long way and you've left some clear messages on the trail. But now the time has come for the big deal.' He paused to study the end of his cigar. 'Some of you boys have been with me quite a long time and I've paid you well.'

He paused again and a low ripple of laughter passed among the men. Jude was studying them carefully and they were a mixed bunch, men like Long Hair and some Mexicans or Indians, and some uncertain about who or what they were. There were at least six he hadn't seen before. They had been out on some nefarious mission with Long Hair, he surmised.

Nolan resumed. 'I have news that the Sullivan boys are due in town today or tomorrow, and they're a real wild bunch. Those Sullivans have one ambition and that's to take over all my interests in town and bury us once and for all up on Boot Hill.'

There was another ripple of laughter and one voice rang out louder than the rest and it was Long Hair. 'OK, so what do we do, boss?'

Nolan pointed his cigar at Long Hair. 'What we do, sir, is we ride right into town and we face up to those scaramouches and make them lick our boots.'

There was another round of laughter. 'That's a good deal,' a man shouted. 'My boots are in need of a clean.'

Another man from closer to the door roared out, 'What are we waiting for, Mr Nolan? What are we waiting for?'

'What's the pay dirt, Mr Nolan?' another man shouted.

Nolan raised his cigar again and jabbed it towards the man who had spoken. 'The pay is twice what you're getting now and anything you can grab from any of those Sullivans you happen to bring down.'

Plus the chance to die in your boots, Jude thought. He glanced at Josh and Josh raised an eyebrow.

'When do we ride, Mr Nolan?' Long Hair shouted.

Nolan consulted his cigar again. 'Well, boys, that's a good question. Jake and his good daughter Nancy will serve up a meal fit for the gods around midday. That will give you time to check your hardware. Then we'll ride into town like the gods from on high and teach those Sullivans a lesson they'll never forget.'

'That's because they'll be stone dead!' a man shouted, and there was a bloodcurdling cheer.

Jude and Josh went back to their quarters to check their weapons. They both had their six-shooters and Josh had his scattergun, the one that had killed the man sneaking up on them by the river.

'What are we gonna do, my friend?' Jude asked Josh.

Josh paused to look down at his gear. 'That's a very good question, Mr James and I'm not sure I know the answer.'

'You don't need to ride into town with the rest of us,' Jude said. 'With that wound in your right shoulder how could you handle a gun?'

Josh rolled his shoulder and flexed his fingers. 'I believe I could manage well enough,' he told Jude. 'Anyways, I could shoot with my left hand. I'm sort of two handed.'

'I think the word you're looking for ambidextrous,' Jude said.

'Well, that's what I am,' Josh agreed.

Jude frowned. 'You don't need to come, my friend. You could stay behind and ride off with that young woman Nancy. That's what the old man wants.'

'I don't think I can do that, Mr James.'

'Why not, if that's what you want?'

'I believe it's a matter of honour,' he said.

'Where's the honour in getting yourself killed?' Jude asked.

Josh gave him that square honest look. 'The honour is when we rode West together we made us an unspoken pact, a partnership, in fact. I don't mean to break that pact.'

Jude gave him an equally square look. 'Well, then, if you mean to come to that hell hole and risk your life, the best thing you can do is to go talk to Nancy before we leave. Give her something to remember you by and give her some hope too. If you don't come back in one piece, at least she'll have at least one good memory.'

Josh smiled. 'I think you're right, Mr James, I think you're right.'

The whole bunch assembled shortly before midday and Nancy and her father dished out the food. When Josh reached the serving point he pushed a bandanna towards Nancy and spoke quietly to her, 'I want you to take this, Miss Nancy, as a token of my regard. I don't have much to give, no gold or silver, but please accept this bandanna as a mark of my respect and my intention towards you.'

Nancy reached out and took the scarf. 'Why, thank you, Mr Appleseed.' She smiled. 'And please come back safe.'

'I'll do my best, Miss Nancy. I'll sure do my best.'

Josh took his plate which was loaded really high and went over to the table to eat.

Jude noticed three things: the first was that Nancy blushed up like a wild red rose; the second was that Jake smiled briefly; the third, and not quite so promising was that Long Hair was sneering in Josh's direction. When it happens, he thought,

97

I'm going to have you clearly in my sights, you long-haired skookum!

The whole bunch mounted up and Jude counted twelve – a good dozen, he thought, not counting Nolan who rode at the head of the column like Caesar or Napoleon. And we all know what happened to them, he reflected with a shudder.

As they rode out Jude saw Nancy and her father waving them off and Nancy was holding up the bright red bandanna Josh had given her.

That man doesn't have a bean to his name, he thought, and neither have I, but there's always a future as long as you survive.

He and Josh was riding together as usual.

'You know what you're doing, man?' he said to Josh.

Josh was smiling to himself. 'Oh, I know well enough,' he laughed, 'and I believe the gods are looking down at me with a smile. You know that feeling, Mr James?'

'I know the feeling, in theory, Mr Appleseed, but I can't claim to have experienced it too often.'

'Oh, you will, you will,' Josh sang out. 'You will, Mr James.'

As they rode along the trail towards town they passed one or two travellers, some riding towards town and others riding out. When they came upon several men riding out of town alone, Nolan held up his arm and drew his small cavalcade to a halt.

'Hi there, Mr Nolan,' one of the travellers greeted.

'Well, hi there, Ned,' Nolan said brightly. 'How are things in town this afternoon?'

'Things are bad,' the traveller said. 'Those Sullivans rode in first thing this morning and I think they got word that you were riding in to challenge them.'

Nolan laughed. 'Is that so, Ned? Did you happen to notice how many there were?'

'I believe I counted twenty,' another man crowed. 'And they look sort of determined, if you know what I mean.'

'Twenty, you say,' Nolan rejoined. 'You sure that was the right number?'

'Can't be certain,' the man said. 'Maybe it was more.'

'That's why we're leaving town, Mr Nolan,' the man called Ned replied. 'We don't want to be caught up in any gunplay with those skunks. We got too much to live for.'

'I'm sure you do,' Nolan said. 'Good day to you boys.' He raised his big black hat politely and the cavalcade rode on.

A little closer to town Jude saw two riders approaching and he recognized them immediately. One was the dark, crow-like figure of Reverend Jerry and the other was the rather overweight town sheriff. The two men reined in and waited as Nolan and his men approached. Then the reverend held up his hand.

'Good day to you, Mr Nolan!' he called.

'Good day, Reverend Jerry,' Nolan replied, none too enthusiastically. 'So I see you're still in town, sir.'

Reverend Jerry beamed a smile at him. 'Thought it was my duty to stick around,' he sang out, 'especially as the good people of this town want to live in peace with the world.'

The sheriff wasn't smiling and he didn't bother to greet Nolan. He said, 'I thought I warned you, Brod Nolan. The people of this town don't need you here with your armed gang. We want peace and prosperity. You bring war and killing and nobody here wants that.'

Jude looked at the short stocky man sitting in the saddle and suddenly felt a surge of admiration towards him. He might not be the best of lawmakers but he was anxious to do his job and earn his meagre wage and he had courage. Jude also had admiration for Reverend Jerry who smiled through all difficulties as though he believed the world of men was fundamentally benevolent.

Nolan stirred in the saddle. 'You say you want peace, Sheriff,' he said. 'I believe we all want peace, peace to get on with our business unmolested.'

'Then why do you bring in your men armed for war?' the sheriff asked him.

Nolan gave a throaty chuckle. 'That's just a precaution, Sheriff, in case we meet some skookums intent on causing a ruckus of some kind.'

'I think I should warn you, Mr Nolan, the Sullivans are in town and they're all armed to the teeth. And they know you're on your way.'

'Well then,' Nolan said, 'I think you made my point for me. Those men want to drive an honest man out of town and that honest man won't agree to that. When you meet evil face to face you have to stare it in the eye and defy it. Otherwise it spreads like the plagues of Egypt and kills the whole community.'

'He's got a point there,' Josh mumbled to Jude.

'Sure, he's got a point. Unfortunately, it isn't good against evil here. It's devil against devil,' Jude replied.

'Like two demons clashing their horns together,' Josh agreed. 'And both might be gored to death.'

For a moment nobody spoke, but Jude could feel tension tight as a bowstring among the men.

Then the reverend spoke up again. 'Mr Nolan, I have a suggestion.'

Nolan glanced back at his men as if looking for support. 'Well now, Mr Jerry, I'm always interested in hearing suggestions, so why don't you spit it out?'

There was a murmur of laughter among the men.

The reverend seemed to gather strength from somewhere. 'Why don't you and your boys just wait here while I ride back into town to talk to those Sullivans? Maybe I could persuade them to leave town or at least come and parley with you.'

Nolan threw back his head and gave a loud bellow of laughter. 'Well, that's the richest thing I've heard in years,' he said. Then he turned to his troops. 'Don't you think that's rich, boys?'

'That's about the richest thing I ever heard,' Long Hair shouted.

The boys gave a loud shout of approval that must have been heard all the way to town and back.

'We've got ourselves into a damned fool position here,' Josh muttered to Jude.

'You spoke about honour,' Jude said. 'I don't think there's much honour here. There's murderous hearts and downright stupidity, that's all.'

'I believe you're right,' Josh said.

'That Dean Sullivan isn't gonna parley with any man,' Nolan said. 'He's a damned sight too mean to parley with the Archangel Gabriel himself.'

That gave rise to another burst of laughter.

'So you're intent on riding on come what may?' Reverend Jerry said.

'I'm intent on riding into this town, half of which I own,' Nolan said. He turned in the saddle and raised his arm. 'Come on, boys, we've got work to do.'

Then he jigged his horse forward and rode on into town.

CHAPTER EIGHT

As they rode on towards Main Street Nolan was looking ahead like a brigadier general.

'You know what, Mr James?' Josh said.

'I'm not sure I do, Mr Appleseed,' Jude said. 'But I do know one thing.'

'The thing I'm thinking, Mr James,' Josh said, 'is that these are just about the worst tactics I can think of. Riding down Main Street like the Grand Old Duke of York and his five thousand men, except the we're not riding up hill and down hill again, and we're only ten, and we're riding down Main Street in full view, and there's no sign of the enemy who might be as many as twenty concealed behind every god-damned window.'

'True, Mr Appleseed, true, and you know why that is, I guess.'

'That's because those Sullivan boys are not dumb enough to ride out to meet us. They prefer to take cover and wait for us to come to them.'

'Good thinking, Mr Appleseed.' Jude was no military tactician but he thought it was damned foolishness to ride into a trap that was about to spring tight on whatever lay between its jaws. He was about to warn Nolan when Reverend Jerry drew in between Josh and him.

'Are you boys quite intent on suicide?' the preacher asked quietly.

'Suicide is not my intent,' Josh replied. 'I'm just doing what I have to do.'

Jerry looked at him askance. 'You've still got your arm in a sling. How can a one-armed man hope to defend himself?'

Josh was thinking about how he could reply when Nolan held up his arm again and the whole contingent came to a halt. They were right on the edge of town and there was a shimmering haze over Main Street. It had been warm all day and now the heat was becoming unbearable. There was even a rumble of thunder over towards the west as though the gods themselves were becoming restless and uneasy about things happening below. But there was no sign of life along Main Street apart from a single mangy cur limping towards the shade of a ramada.

The whole cavalcade stood and waited, but it was as though the town was taking its afternoon siesta or had died.

'I don't like the sound of that,' Jude said to Josh.

'That's the buzz of silence,' Josh replied, 'and it's a lot too loud for me.'

'That, my friend, is also the sound of death,' the preacher announced grimly. 'The grim reaper is waiting behind every window and every door in this town. He's licking his chops and cocking his gun and just waiting for you men to come within his sights. And his name in this case is Dean Sullivan.'

'Well, it's good of you to warn us, Mr Preacher,' Josh said. 'That's just what we need at this time.'

Nolan looked thoughtful. He had stopped to light up one of those fat Havana cigars of his and he turned to face his troops. He still looked like Napoleon except that Napoleon didn't smoke cigars; he just breathed fire and brimstone.

'Now, boys,' Nolan said, 'we have a slight change of plan. Those Sullivans don't play by the rules. None of them is man enough to ride to meet us down Main Street. Their balls are too weak and too flabby for that.'

That gave rise to more laughter, some of it more than a little apprehensive.

'So what we must do is dismount and root out those bastards house by house. We make a remuda and Carlos will be wrangler until we've got ourselves clear of this business.'

'That sounds like better tactics,' Josh said.

'Jed Oliphant will take the left-hand side of Main Street,' Nolan ordered, 'and I will take the right.' He then detailed off the men who would go with him and those who would go with Jed Oliphant. Josh and Jude would take the right side of Main Street with Nolan two other *hombres*, which was fine by them since they didn't trust Long Hair Oliphant any further than they could throw him.

The boys dismounted and led their horses to a water trough right on the edge of town where the Mexican Carlos the wrangler would take care of them.

That makes five of us on this side,' Josh said. 'The odds aren't by any means great in our favour, are they, Mr James?'

'That depends on where those Sullivans have decided to squat down,' Jude replied. He was beginning to like this operation less and less. He took his Winchester out of its sheath and checked it over. 'Keep that scattergun ready,' he said to Josh. 'It could be useful at close quarters. That's if you can hold it steady with that bad arm of yours.'

Josh took his arm out of its sling and held the shotgun up as if to prove he could fire it. Then he eased his Colt in its holster. 'I don't figure that will be too much trouble, Mr James,' he said.

Jude nodded. 'I have a suggestion, Mr Appleseed.'

'And what's that, Mr James?'

'If we're going to go through with this damned foolishness, I think we should stick together whatever may happen.'

'I agree to that, Mr James.' Josh held out his left hand and squeezed Jude's arm.

The Reverend Jerry and the sheriff were still on their horses conferring together. The sheriff turned to Nolan and said, 'In the name of the law I'm telling you to stay where you are and hold your fire till we've talked to the Sullivans. Give us ten minutes to see what we can fix.'

'You're wasting your time!' Nolan shouted. 'But I'm gonna enjoy this good Havana cigar. Then I'm gonna walk down to The Grand Hotel and order a meal. That's what I'm gonna do.'

'Well, if you're intent on getting yourself killed, that's your business,' the sheriff said. 'They tell me the devil does a great line in steaks and you'd better enjoy it because it might be your last meal on earth.'

'I think that's meant to be some kind of joke,' Josh muttered to Jude. 'I didn't figure the sheriff for being a great humorist but you learn something every day.'

'In this kind of situation,' Jude replied, 'some men crack jokes and some shit their pants,' Jude said, 'and he prefers to laugh.'

'Well, then, I guess we should be thankful for the jokes,' Josh replied.

Nolan raised his hand and signalled to Jed Oliphant who started across Main Street with his four companions. The idea was that the two parties should keep pace with each other, building by building, to flush out the opposition.

'I don't think the Emperor Napoleon would have done it this way,' Josh said to Jude.

'Napoleon wasn't so great,' Jude murmured quietly. 'Look what happened after he attacked that city in Russia. What was it called?'

'That was Moscow, I believe,' Josh said. 'And I believe he lost most of his army on the way back.'

'It doesn't look good, man,' Jude agreed.

War is an occupation for fools. Jude thought, as they began to edge down the sidewalk from building to building.

Nolan held up his arm and waved them to silence. He looked across Main Street and saw Jed Oliphant and his four *compadres* inching along opposite, but between them the sheriff and Reverend Jerry were riding their horses slowly and carefully as though they were leading some kind of dignified parade.

The town was as dead as a dodo and as hot as the hobs of Hell. All the good people were either hiding under their beds or crouching behind tables in their rooms, hoping for the best outcome. Somewhere towards the back of the second building Jude heard the distant wailing of a child. For some reason he suddenly thought of that young woman Sarah Jane waving to him from behind a curtain on the upper floor of The Grand Hotel.

Then something unexpected happened. A door further along Main Street was pushed open and a man stumbled out as though thrust by a hidden gun. He turned as if to protest and than stepped onto Main Street and raised his hands. 'Don't shoot!' he said in a voice edged with panic. Jude recognized the gnome-like figure immediately: it was Gullivant, the store keeper, but his cheeks weren't quite as cherubic and rosy as usual. He turned to listen to a voice coming from inside the store, then looked towards Nolan. 'Mr Nolan!' he shouted in a quavering voice. 'Don't shoot! I have to talk to you!'

106

Nolan said nothing. He stepped to the edge of the sidewalk and beckoned the man forward.

Gullivant came shambling towards him, still with his hands raised. He was wearing his blue striped apron. 'Mr Nolan,' he repeated tremulously. 'They sent me out with a message.'

Nolan took his cigar from his mouth and breathed out a cloud of smoke. 'What's the message?' he asked.

Gullivant stumbled forward a pace or two. 'It's my wife,' he said. 'They're holding her in the store.'

Nolan tapped the ash from the end of his cigar. 'Your wife,' he repeated without emotion.

'Yes, sir, my wife and a number of other ladies. Those Sullivans are holding them hostage in the store.'

'I'm real sorry to hear that, Mr Gullivant, real sorry. And what's the message?'

The poor man's lips trembled as he tried to reply. 'The Sullivans say if you don't get out of town in five minutes they're going to. . . .' Jude saw tears in the man's eyes as he tried to go on.

'Going to what?' Nolan asked through tight lips.

Gullivant tried to pull himself together. 'I think they mean to kill my wife, Mr Nolan.'

Nolan rolled his cigar between his fingers. 'Well now, Mr Gullivant,' he said, 'you go right back and tell those yellow-bellied skookums that if they harm any of those women, they'll hang high on the gallows before the end of this day.'

Gullivant's lips worked without saying anything for a moment or two. Then he half whispered, 'I think those Sullivans mean it, sir.'

Nolan looked at Jude. 'You see what we're dealing with here, Mr James? Those Sullivans aren't men, they're blood-crazed monsters.' He turned to the cringing wreck of a man. 'How many of those Sullivans are in the store, Mr Gullivant?'

Gullivant seemed dazed. 'There's maybe three or four,' he said. 'Most of the others are in The Grand Hotel. But they seem to be all over town. I don't rightly know how many there are.'

Jude froze. Inside The Grand Hotel, he thought. That's where that young woman Sarah Jane is.

'Mr Gullivant, I want you to go right back to your store and do what I say. Tell the Sullivans that if they let those women go free they might live to see another day. If not they'll be dead meat hanging from the gallows.'

'So that's your reply, Mr Nolan?' Gullivant said.

'That's my reply,' Nolan agreed.

Then Josh spoke up. 'This man's fit to fall,' he said. 'Why don't I go and deliver your message for you? I could keep my arm in the sling and they'll think I'm about as good as a dead duck.'

Nolan opened his eyes wide in amazement. 'How do you think that will help, Mr Appleseed?' he asked. 'It sounds like nothing but foolishness to me.'

'I could tell them that there's no hope in this. We're in a dead end situation here and, if they don't see reason, there are going to be a whole lot of corpses littering the street here before sundown.'

Nolan grinned. 'You've got grit, Mr Appleseed, just like I said but I don't think things work out like that. As soon as you step into that store you'll be shot down before you can open your mouth and take in enough breath to speak.'

Josh was just about to reply when there was the sound of a shot from the direction of Gullivant's store.

'Oh, my God!' Gullivant screamed. 'They've shot my wife!'

In fact the shot had been fired from the store across Main Street and the sheriff jerked and slid from his horse to the ground. Reverend Jerry's horse reared and bolted in the direction of The Grand Hotel.

'My God, that's the sheriff!' Gullivant shouted.

'Hold your fire!' Nolan shouted to his men, but it was too late: Jed Oliphant crouched behind a sidewalk post and fired a shot towards the store.

'So the fun begins!' Josh said. 'The bung is out of the bottle and the wine will start to gush!'

Jude was looking towards the sheriff and saw him twitch and move and try to get to his feet. But then a whole fusillade of shots rang out between the store and Nolan's men on the opposite side of the street. It was difficult to see what was happening because of the smoke and the dust.

'The sheriff isn't dead,' Jude shouted. 'Look, he's crawling towards the sidewalk to get himself under cover.'

It was a ridiculous but pathetic sight; a man dragging himself through the dust hoping to save his life.

'By Jehosaphat!' Josh said. 'There's Doc Winter, going to help him!'

The doc had suddenly emerged waving a white bandanna and shouting to everyone to hold their fire.

There was a temporary cessation of fire. The doc ran out and bent over the victim and tried to examine him, but then a hot-head from further along Main Street fired a couple of shots and all hell broke out again.

'Wish me luck,' Jude said to Josh.

'What in hell are you going to do?' Josh said between his teeth.

'I'm going out there to get the sheriff under cover,' Jude said.

Before Josh had a chance to restrain him Jude ran towards Doc Winter and the wounded man.

Josh muttered to himself, 'That man's nothing but a damned fool,' but he too rushed out, shouting wildly and waving his shotgun.

Doc Winter looked up in amazement. 'This man's badly wounded. If we don't get him under cover he'll be hit again.'

Jude saw that the sheriff was hit high in the chest and there was blood spurting from his mouth. Moving him might actually kill him but they had to take the risk. So he grabbed the sheriff's arm and started to haul him towards the sidewalk. The wounded man cried out in agony and passed out.

'Steady, steady,' said Doc Winter.

Josh was suddenly like a raging bull. He turned to face the store and fired his shotgun, but the range was too great. So he threw the shotgun down and drew his Colt and fired several shots at the men crouching by the doorway under the ramada. One of Sullivan's men pitched forward on to the sidewalk and the other took a shot and disappeared inside the store.

Now Long Hair Oliphant emerged from the shadows and tried to grab at the sheriff's body.

'Leave him!' Doc Winter warned. 'There's nothing more we can do. He's about to die.'

As if in response, the sheriff opened his eyes. He gasped and tried to speak, but the blood gushed from his lips and he fell back dead.

The doctor looked across at the store. 'That's what you get for trying to bring peace,' he gasped. 'He was a brave man and he didn't deserve this.'

Josh was down on one knee, steadying his revolver. Then he stood up and ran towards the store.

'Your partner must be crazy,' the doc said to Jude. 'by rights his shoulder should have given out by now.'

'He is crazy,' Jude said. 'And I'm going over there to join him before he gets himself killed.' He darted across the street just as one of the windows was smashed and a gun poked out.

It was pointed right at him, but before the gunman could open fire Josh pistol whipped his wrist so that it came down on the broken glass. There was a scream from inside and Josh fired a shot through the window which found its mark.

Jude ran on and crouched beside Josh. 'What are we going to do?' he asked.

'We have to get those women out alive,' Josh said.

But now there was a diversion. From further along Main Street towards The Grand Hotel figures had started to emerge.

'They're coming out like rats from a sinking ship,' Nolan said from behind Jude.

'Rats with sharp teeth,' Jude said. 'And the ship isn't quite sinking yet.'

'That is a complication,' Josh agreed, 'but I want to get those women out of here.'

Nolan nodded. 'Well, that's right. I've sent the other two boys round to the back to smoke those bastards out.'

'Well, here we go then!' Josh stood up and kicked at the door. He had a good strong leg and the door collapsed inward. A shot came from inside but it missed Josh by inches since he had crouched low close to the wall. There were screams from inside and then the women rushed out. Nolan grabbed Gullivant's wife and dragged her to safety. One of the other women, a stout lady in her fifties, rushed out surprisingly fast and tripped and fell on the sidewalk, and another woman trying to push past her, tripped and fell over her. A fourth woman darted to one side and collapsed on the sidewalk.

'That's the ladies dealt with!' Josh shouted, and he rushed into the store with his Colt cocked and ready. Jude followed him with his own weapon held out but there was no one inside. Sullivan's men had retreated to the back. Next second there was the noise of heavy gunfire from behind the store.

'Let's get those ladies to safety!' Jude said.

Josh wasn't sure. He wanted to rampage through the store and shoot at the Sullivans as they retreated.

'Hold your fire, boys!' Nolan commanded. 'See those ladies back out of range.'

Gullivant, the store keeper, suddenly appeared from behind them and he rushed forward to grab his wife. But she didn't need much encouragement to get up and scramble to safety.

Now attention turned to the end of Main Street where the hordes of Sullivan were advancing.

'Maybe they've got more balls than I figured,' Nolan said, as he checked his Winchester. 'Don't waste ammunition, boys. At this distance you'd be lucky if you winged an elephant.' He signalled to Jed Oliphant and he and his team prepared to meet the oncoming gunmen who were now almost close enough to take a shot at.

But there were complications in the shape of Doc Winter, who was still on Main Street, and Reverend Jerry who had mastered his horse and was riding back between the warring parties towards Nolan and his men. When he got close enough he waved his arms and shouted something.

'That mad preacher is trying to tell us something,' Nolan laughed. 'I don't think those scaramouches will think twice about blasting him from his saddle even if he is a so-called *holy man*.'

Yet, as the preacher rode on there was no firing from the Sullivans. They just kept on coming with their weapons raised.

'Maybe they think he's some sort of holy angel,' Josh suggested.

The Reverend Jerry rode right up to them and dismounted.

'Mr Nolan,' he said, 'I beg you to stop this bloodshed before it gets out of hand. Those Sullivans are quite ruthless, but I believe you are a man of peace. You can stop this nonsense before more men and women are killed.'

Nolan still had his cigar clenched between his teeth. 'You're right, Reverend Jerry, I am a man of peace, but when the chips are down you have to be ready to fight to protect yourself. That's what life is about.'

'How many of those Sullivans are there?' Jude asked.

The preacher pointed towards the advancing men. 'I see ten men coming towards you, but there are more. By my reckoning you are outnumbered by at least two to one. There's a whole lot more in the hotel . . . I don't know how many.'

Nolan bit hard on his cigar. 'My guess is they've been drinking too,' he said. 'What d'you expect me to do, Reverend? Call my boys off and crawl away with my tail between my legs?'

The Reverend Jerry didn't know how to answer that. 'Maybe we could arrive at some sort of compromise,' he said without conviction.

Nolan gave a sceptical grunt. Then he took the stub of his cigar out of his mouth and threw it down. As he did so there was an ominous rumbling sound from the west where the clouds were piling like high cauliflowers in the sky.

'There's gonna be a storm, Mr Appleseed,' Jude said.

'A mighty big one too,' Josh agreed.

There was a shot from the Sullivans and, a moment later, a bullet whined past Jude so close it almost clipped his ear. He ducked down and grabbed his Winchester.

'That was a Sharps Big Fifty,' Nolan said, 'used for buffalo hunting.'

'Well, I'm no buffalo,' Jude said, 'but now I have some notion of what they feel like when that gun is aimed at them.'

Josh raised his Colt and held it steady. 'I'm thinking of what might have happened way back there,' he said, referring to the store. Everything had gone deadly quiet in the store. Either Nolan's two men had shot down the Sullivans trying to escape, or they had themselves been shot down which meant that there were only three men on this side of the street to face the oncoming horde. Long Hair Oliphant and his team were no more than five, which made eight – eight against ten, not counting however many there were holed up in The Grand Hotel.

Nolan signalled to Jed Oliphant again. 'Keep down and let them come to you!' he said.

Oliphant raised his arm and signalled back. Though he was a braggart and a bully, he knew one or two things about tactics.

As the men came on Jude recognized Dean Sullivan. He was standing right in the middle of the street, holding up the Sharps Big Fifty. Then he shouted, and he had a really strong, deep voice.

'Listen, Nolan, I have a suggestion. You want to hear it?'

Nolan was about to light another of those Havana cigars but he stopped dead and looked directly at his enemy. 'What's your suggestion, Sullivan?' he yelled.

Sullivan cupped his mouth with his hand and shouted even louder. 'I've been talking to the reverend here and I think he's right about one thing: we don't need to shed any unnecessary blood. So, why don't we call a halt? Then you and me walk down Main Street and shoot it out between us just like they do over in Europe some place. One shot each with our Colt pistols and the best man wins.'

'What happens to the man who loses?'

'Well, I guess he hasn't too much to worry about because he'll be dead.'

There was a rumble of laughter from both sides, followed by an even louder rumble from the approaching clouds. Jude noticed that both Preacher Jerry and Doc Winter had disappeared and there were no stray dogs in evidence either.

Nolan stuck his new cigar in his mouth and worked his brow and for a moment said nothing. Then he turned to Jude. 'You know what I think?'

'I guess you're going to tell me, anyway,' Jude said.

Nolan grunted. 'You see what's happening? Those Sullivan desperadoes are melting away like rabbits. I have a feeling those in the store are loose somewhere behind us. Dean Sullivan is just stalling for time. If I go out there and face him there's someone behind a window up there just waiting to shoot me down.'

Jude looked up from behind the sidewalk overhang and saw a curtain fluttering from an open window on the opposite side of Main Street. 'I think you're right,' he said.

'I'm damned sure I'm right,' Nolan said.

Then Dean Sullivan spoke again. 'So you ain't saying a lot, Nolan,' he said. 'Does that mean you don't know what to say, or you haven't got the *cojones* to step out and take my challenge?'

Nolan was still biting on his cigar but he hadn't lit it yet, then suddenly made up his mind. He snatched the cigar from his mouth and handed it to Jude – who wasn't too pleased to accept it.

'OK, Sullivan, I'll take your challenge but on one condition.'

'What?' Sullivan asked warily.

'We ask Doc Winter and the Reverend Jerry to act as referees.'

Sullivan looked somewhat perplexed. He nodded and held his head on one side.

There was another rumble of thunder even closer.

'Keep talking, Mr Nolan,' Josh said. 'I think the gods are taking a hand in this. They might even strike Sullivan down with a bolt of lightning. I've seen it happen once or twice.'

But before the gods could intervene someone more earthly took a hand. Whoever was behind that fluttering curtain above got tired of waiting and fired a shot.

The bullet hit a post no more than an inch to the right of Nolan's head. Nolan ducked down.

Josh took up a Winchester and fired at the man behind the open window and the man reared back and disappeared. 'I think I got him,' Josh said.

'Well, you sure got something,' Jude said, as gunfire erupted from both sides of the street and from windows and roof tops. Dean Sullivan fired a couple of wild shots in Nolan's direction and then ran towards a ramada further up the street.

'So that's Sullivan's idea of a fair gunfight,' Josh shouted. He was really fired up and ready for battle.

'Keep your head down!' Jude warned him.

He should have said it to Jed Oliphant who stepped out to take a shot at Dean Sullivan. Then he jerked with an expression of amazement and fell on to his back.

'I think we lost Oliphant,' Josh speculated.

'I think you're right,' Jude said. Jed Oliphant was lying as still as an ancient monument with his gun still in his hand.

'What do we do now?' Josh asked.

Nolan was bristling. 'Those Sullivans are not gonna drive me out of my own town!' he roared. 'I made it and it belongs to me!' Holding his Colt low he started along the sidewalk towards where Sullivan and disappeared.

Jude and Josh exchanged sceptical looks.

'Looks like we're walking into hell itself,' Josh said.

'Well, there sure are plenty of devils around,' Jude replied, 'but as long as we keep ourselves under the ramada on the sidewalk those yellow bellies in the windows above can't get a bead on us. I guess the Sullivans didn't think much about that.'

Nolan now waved across for the others to follow, but would they obey or had they got cold feet? Jed Oliphant still hadn't moved.

CHAPTER NINE

Nolan ran on and Jude and Josh followed him, pausing behind each ground-floor window and door, checking that there weren't any more devils waiting inside. But they saw no devils. All they saw were terrified men, women, and children peering out at them, desperate to survive. Then Josh opened a door and walked into a house. A woman screamed and two frightened children ducked down behind an upturned table.

'Hush there!' Josh said. 'No need to be afraid. Me and my buddy don't want to harm you. We're here to look after you.'

The woman peeped out at him and pleaded. 'Don't harm my children, mister. We're good people. We never did anyone any harm.'

'I'm sure that's true, ma'am,' Josh assured her. 'I just want to go upstairs and look across the street. You don't happen to have any gunmen up there, do you, ma'am?'

'I don't think so, sir,' she said.

'You mind if we take a look see?' Josh asked her.

The woman made a strange motion towards the upstairs with her head.

'OK, ma'am,' Josh said. 'You just bide here.'

'Don't get yourself killed,' the woman said.

Josh gave Jude a wry look and then went on to the stairs. 'Stay here,' he said to Jude. 'This is my fight.'

'I don't think so,' Jude said. 'Nolan can take care of himself. I'm coming up with you.,

'Let's take it quietly then,' Josh advised.

They tiptoed up the stairs to the landing. Josh turned and signed Jude to keep quiet. Then he turned the handle of the door and peered inside. There were two men at the window and both were too busy firing at Nolan's men to notice Josh and Jude.

Josh raised his Colt and brought it right down on a man's head and the man slumped forward on to the sill.

The other man, a big bearded fellow, turned quickly and lunged out and Josh fell to the floor. The bearded man then took a swing at Jude but Jude was ready. The swing went wide and Jude struck the man between the eyes with his left fist. The man fell back against the window and then came forward again with a roar, trying to get his Winchester round.

Jude grabbed the Winchester and wrenched it away. Then he struck out at the man with his fist again. The man was big and as strong as an ox. He lashed out at Jude and caught him on the chin. Jude fell back against a bed and the bearded man sprang on to him with a roar. The bed collapsed and both men rolled off it on to the floor.

The bearded man was up first. 'I'm gonna kill you!' he shouted. 'I'm gonna lick the living daylights out of you!'

He should have saved his breath because Jude rolled over and leaped to his feet. As the big man lumbered in, Jude struck out with his fists. The first blow connected with the man's midriff. The second struck him on the point of the jaw. The man staggered back towards the open window and pitched over the sill and disappeared with a yell.

Jude went to the window and watched as the man hit the

119

ramada, rolled to the edge, and pitched backwards to the street below.

'That didn't do him one little bit of good,' Josh said. 'Where did you learn that trick?'

'Came to me naturally, Mr Appleseed.'

They looked down at the man Josh had felled and the man didn't stir.

'He's gonna have an awful bad head when he comes round,' Jude said.

'That's if he does come round,' Josh surmised.

They dragged the man away from the window and Josh retrieved his weapon. 'Useful shooter, this. I think I might take a pop at those skookums in the opposite window.'

'That's one way of helping our lord and master Mr Nolan,' Jude said, 'and I reckon he's going to need all the help he can get.'

'You're damn right on that.' Josh cocked the gun and knelt at the window searching for a likely target, and he didn't have long to wait. There were several windows just to the right where gunmen were steadying their weapons, scanning for targets in the street below.

There was one gunman on a roof looking down from the façade. Jude levelled his Winchester and squeezed the trigger. The man seemed to look up at the sky as though searching for a bird, then he pitched back and disappeared. 'Good night, gentlemen! Good night!' Jude said.

'Good shooting too!' Josh commented. 'You deserve a medal, Mr James.' He raised the Winchester and squeezed the trigger. The gun jerked back against his shoulder but nobody fell in the opposite window. 'That's some recoil,' he said.

'Should keep them busy though,' Jude rejoined.

Then a couple of incoming shots smashed against the raised window and splintered glass came showering down on Josh's head. 'Good job I had my hat on,' he remarked.

'The lady isn't gonna like this one little bit,' Jude observed. 'What with the ruined bed and a smashed-up window, not to mention that poleaxed villain lying there on the bedroom floor.'

'Maybe we should heave him out of the window or prop him up so they can use him for target practice. What do you think, Mr James?'

'I think you should stay here and keep them busy while I go down and apologize for any inconvenience,' Jude said.

'Apologies aren't gonna get you anywhere,' Josh reasoned. 'What those poor people need is recompense and a new bed.'

Jude worked his way down the stairs and into the room below where the woman and the kids were still taking cover where they could. When they saw Jude they cowered back as though he was about to shoot them.

'Don't worry, ma'am,' Jude tried to reassure the woman. 'We don't mean you any harm. Josh is a peace-loving man and I wouldn't harm a single being unless I had to.'

'Are you Mr Nolan's men?' the woman asked timorously.

'We're our own men, ma'am. Mr Nolan hired us but we know our own minds. Right now we're trying to rid the town of the Sullivans.'

The woman leaned forward from her hiding place. 'When is this going to end?' she implored.

'I'm afraid I can't answer that, ma'am. I guess it will end when there are no more bully boys around.'

'That won't be till the end of time,' the woman said.

'True, ma'am, true,' Jude agreed. He saw that the woman was no more than thirty and even younger looking when she smiled. 'I want to apologize for the mess upstairs,'! he said.

'There's a smashed window and a few bullet holes up there. And, I'm sorry to say, a wrecked bed too. I'll make sure you get paid to put things right.'

'Thank you, sir,' she said humbly. 'We just want it to end.'

Jude nodded. He thought of his own folk, how poor they had been. 'Now I'm just going out by the back way. My partner Josh will be sitting in that window a bit longer, if you don't mind.'

'You take care, sir,' the woman said.

'And when I leave, I suggest you lock the doors and keep as quiet as you can because those skookums will want revenge for what we've done to them.'

Jude went out by the backdoor and found himself in a narrow back yard with a small wooden fence. He looked left and right and froze. Not more than fifty feet to the right he saw two men moving close to the cabins in his direction. That gave him the answer he had been looking for: the two Nolan men who had gone through the house closer to the remuda had been killed or wounded, which meant that Nolan's cavalcade had been severely reduced. It looked as though he and Josh were in an extremely tight spot. He levelled his Winchester and took a bead on the first man. And then the man saw him and dodged back into a doorway. The second man followed quickly.

What do I do now? Jude wondered. The answer came immediately. A revolver came round the corner and took a shot in his direction. It was a blind shot but it gave the gunman the chance he needed. He darted across the yard and dived behind an outhouse. Jude took a shot at him and missed. Then he levered his Winchester and waited.

The second man pushed out a hat, but Jude still waited. I'm not falling for that trick, he thought.

Then the first man took another shot at him from behind the door of the outhouse. Instead of retreating, Jude ran towards it and took a couple of shots. The door swung back and the gunman disappeared. The second gunman suddenly appeared with a Colt bucking in his hand. He fired two shots and came on recklessly towards Jude. Jude levered his Winchester frantically but it was empty!

The second gunman crouched and cocked his Colt.

Jude hurled his Winchester straight at the man's head and the man ducked, which gave Jude time to draw his own Colt. But, before he could fire, the man raised his hands and shouted, 'All right! You win!'

'Then throw down your gun and get down on your knees,' Jude said.

The man let his gun drop and knelt down cautiously.

Jude went forward and put his gun to the man's forehead. He could have squeezed the trigger and blown him to Kingdom Come, but he pulled the gun away. 'Did you kill those men back there?' he asked.

'I never killed anyone,' the man stammered. 'I was just defending myself.'

'Hm,' Jude said. His heart was beating fast and he still had half a mind to beat the man over the head with his Colt. The gunman was shivering with terror. 'I'm gonna kill you if I have to,' Jude said. 'Make no mistake about that.'

'You don't have to kill me,' the man whimpered. 'I don't want any part of this. I'm no killer. I just want to be out of this thing.'

'That's a good story,' Jude said. 'Just face the wall and keep quiet, or I will blow your head off.'

The man gave him a sidelong glance and pressed his face to the wall. Jude stooped and retrieved the man's gun and stuffed it through his own belt. He looked past the outhouse but there was no sign of the other gunman. 'OK,' he said. 'Now I want you to walk along in front of me in the direction of the The Grand Hotel. D'you hear me?'

'I hear you,' the man whimpered.

'And if you make a single false move, I shall have to kill you.'

'You don't have to do that, mister,' the man pleaded. 'I work for Mr Sullivan because he pays me, that's all. I never wanted to harm any man or woman.' As he was speaking he glanced quickly towards the outbuilding where the other gunman had taken refuge.

'I just hope your *compadre* is of the same mind,' Jude said.

They walked behind the buildings along Main Street, Jude keeping his gun pressed against the man's back. He could still hear gunfire from Main Street and concluded that the snipers and Josh were still busy. And the clouds were massing to the west of the town. The buildings were spread intermittently. Some were close together and others further apart, which meant traversing open ground.

Quite soon Jude knew they must be approaching The Grand Hotel. That was when he heard shots from close along Main Street and a man came running along the side of a building with a gun in his hand. The man dropped down among a row of cabbages and swivelled round to face an approaching enemy. It was Nolan himself. Then another man rushed into the garden in close pursuit.

'Get yourself down!' Jude ordered his captive. Then he loosed off a shot at the pursuing man. The shot took the man full in the chest and he jerked back and fell with a cry.

Nolan scrambled to his feet and he didn't look quite as cool as usual: his cigar had disappeared.

'Great God!' he said to Jude, 'you saved my life, boy!' He

looked at the captive. 'Is this one of Sullivan's men?'

'I believe it is,' Jude told him.

Nolan seized the captive by the shirt and glared into his face. 'Why, you son of a bitch!' he roared. 'I should kill you right now!'

Jude took Nolan by the arm. 'Hold on there, Mr Nolan! We've got other things to do.'

Nolan slowly released his grip on the man. 'What's your name, son?'

'Panchez,' the man muttered. 'I don't mean you no harm, sir. I just got into this business by accident.'

'Well, Panchez, I've got news for you. You got into this business just in time to be useful.' He pressed the barrel of his gun to the man's head.

'What do you want me to do, sir?' Panchez stammered.

'What you do, Panchez, is you walk along ahead of me just in case Mr Dean Sullivan wants to take a shot at me. You *comprendez?*'

'Yes, sir,' Panchez said. 'That Dean Sullivan is an awful bad man.'

'I know that, Panchez. He's so bad we have to kill him. You understand me?'

'Yes, Mr Nolan.'

'OK.' Nolan grinned malevolently. 'Now I want you to turn around and walk ahead of me, but not too far away. So if one of those Sullivans takes a shot in our direction, you'll be the first to drop. You understand me?'

'I understand you, sir,' the man stammered.

They walked on through the cabbage patch towards the sidewalk on Main Street. Nolan glanced back at Jude and said, 'I won't forget this, Mr James. When we clear out these scumbags you and your buddy will be my top hands.'

'Well, that sounds really generous, Mr Nolan, but we've got

a little way to go before that.'

They paused by the body of the man Jude had shot.

'That was good shooting,' Nolan remarked. 'You shot him stone dead.'

'Well, I'm not gonna cut a notch in my gun,' Jude said, looking at the dead man's contorted face. He felt somewhat nauseous.

They reached the sidewalk on Main Street and turned to the right. Jude looked to the left and saw Josh running towards them under cover of the ramada. 'Here comes my buddy,' he said. 'I think we should wait for him.'

Nolan turned. 'Stop right there!' he said to Panchez. Panchez stopped abruptly no more than five feet away.

Jude watched as Nolan signalled to his two remaining men opposite and they signalled back and stopped. Jude raised his Winchester to cover Josh as he ran across the sidewalk beside the cabbage patch.

'Thought I might catch up with you,' Josh said, gasping for breath.

'How did it go?' Jude asked him.

'Well, I kept their heads down and I think I might have sent one or two more to the great kingdom above or to the dark pit below,' Josh said. 'So I thought I should come along and give you guys a hand.'

'Good work, Mr Appleseed,' Nolan said. 'We're gonna make our way down to The Grand Hotel where the main bunch are holed up.'

'I hope you know what you're doing, Mr Nolan, because it seems there's a lot of them holed up in there, including Dean Sullivan himself.'

'You're probably right,' Nolan admitted, 'but I own that hotel and I'm not gonna let Dean Sullivan grab it and drive me out.'

'Well, if that's what you want, Mr Nolan,' Josh said. He glanced at Jude and gave him what looked like a wink. 'How do you mean to smoke them out, Mr Nolan? You can't walk right in and shoot everybody in sight. As soon as you poke your nose inside that door there'll be someone ready to shoot it right off. I hope you realize that, sir.'

'What we do is we send in Panchez here ahead of us,' Nolan said.

'Is that a good plan, Mr Nolan?' Josh asked.

Panchez half turned and stammered out, 'Dean Sullivan will blast my head off as soon I put it through that door, Mr Nolan.'

'You should have thought about that before you got so deep into this shit,' Nolan said.

But before they could go any further something totally unexpected occurred. The door of the hotel burst open and a man rushed out with his coat tails on fire. It was the butler himself. He rushed across the sidewalk full tilt on to the street. 'Help! Help!' he shouted, 'I'm on fire! Someone help me!' Then he plumped his butt down in the dust and rolled about trying desperately to extinguish the fire.

At that moment there was violent explosion from the ground floor of the hotel and several other flaming figures rushed out screaming with pain.

'My Gawd, the Devil himself has taken a hand!' Josh shouted.

'He's burning down my property!' Nolan complained.

There was a horse trough on the other side of Main Street and someone produced a bucket and started hurling water over the flaming bodies.

Then the Reverend Jerry rode up on his big black horse. He wheeled round with one hand in the air, pointing to the sky. 'That's what you get for killing one another!' he shouted.

'This is madness! Utter madness!' He sounded so distressed that he was close to tears. He leaped from his horse and rushed over to the horse trough, waving his hands in the air. Then he stripped off his long black coat and threw it over the burning man who was still trying to smother the flames on his coat tail. The reverend's black horse reared and bolted down Main Street.

'There's a horse with some horse savvy!' Josh exclaimed.

'What are we gonna do?' Nolan shouted. It was the first time Jude had seen him so alarmed.

Now there was another explosion from the hotel, and then another, and flames started pouring through the windows on the ground floor of the building.

Jude ran. That girl Sarah Jane, he thought, she must be in there. She'll be burned to death! He looked up and there she was behind a window on the second floor, looking down and waving frantically. He couldn't hear what she was saying, but he knew she was begging him to save her. How to save her; that was the problem. Jude's brain raced.

'I've got to save that girl!' he shouted to Josh who had joined him.

'You need to be quick!' Josh shouted back.

Jude looked around, but there was no ladder available. 'Quick!' he said, 'help me to get up on the overhang!'

'Well,' Josh said, 'I'll do my best.' He stretched his good left arm and steadied it against the ramada post. Jude climbed up on to his left shoulder and hauled himself up. They could both feel the heat pulsing from inside the building. The over hang was steep but Jude managed to scramble up, hanging on to whatever he could until he reached a window. 'Climb out!' he said to the girl at the window. 'I've got my hand on the sill and I can get you down, but we need to be quick because the whole place is going up at any second!'

Despite her dark skin, the girl looked as pale as the moon, but she was determined to survive and she soon got herself out of the building.

'Now lie down and slide,' Jude said. 'I can steady you as you come down.'

Sarah Jane didn't need to be told twice. She just lay right down and eased herself to the edge of the overhang where Josh grabbed her ankle.

'Easy does it,' Josh said.

Jude slid down beside her and swung his legs over the edge. It was quite a drop and he knew Josh couldn't help him without his letting go of the girl. So he went over the edge and hoped for the best. Still holding her, he got his knee against the post and knew he could slide on down. At that moment a gust of hot air blew from the entrance of the hotel like a blast from a furnace.

Jude dropped and rolled back and Josh fell, still holding the girl beside him. For a moment Jude lay on his back waiting for the pain to strike. Then he turned to the girl. 'Are you OK?' he managed to say.

Sarah Jane had no time to answer because at that moment strong arms seized her and dragged her away. Josh was on his knees, yelling at no one in particular as he too was dragged to safety.

Jude rolled over and started to crawl across the street. Then the Reverend Jerry was beside him.

'It's gonna be all right!' he was saying.

'It's gonna be all right!' Jude agreed, and it was all right, but not for the town.

The local fire service, such as it was, had managed to get itself together and the part-time firemen were busy passing buckets, but it was too late to save The Grand Hotel. The survivors were on the other side, huddling under the ramada and Doc Winter was doing what he could to help them. Jude, Josh and Sarah Jane sat on the sidewalk doing their best to recover.

Nolan was striding back and forth but he had no cigar in his mouth. He just looked horrified. Then there was a mighty flash of lightning, followed immediately by a huge crash of thunder, and the heavens opened and a deluge came down.

'Is that a present from the Devil or the Almighty Himself?' Josh asked nobody in particular.

CHAPTER TEN

When night cast its wing the town seemed to curl in on itself and go into mourning. There was no more shooting and no more loud cursing. The hotel had burned right down to the ground and taken several adjoining buildings with it. But the rest of the town had mercifully survived, thanks partly to the torrent of rain that came bucketing down after the thunder and lightning.

The dead were carried on makeshift stretchers to the funeral director's yard where they were laid out side by side in rows for identification. Jed Oliphant and the sheriff looked peaceful, but some of the other victims were contorted or had expressions of horror on their dead faces. The remains of the devastated hotel were still smouldering, so it was impossible to estimate how many bodies lay inside. There was no sign of Dean Sullivan.

'That Sullivan has either died in the fire or has been carried away in the arms of the Devil!' Nolan was heard to mutter to himself. Jude thought it was an interesting concept, though, in this case, the Devil had a rather strange sense of discrimination.

Sarah Jane, whom Jude and Josh had saved, was half in despair and half relieved: she had lost several close friends in the conflagration but she was at least alive. The butler and the other men who had rushed out with flames cascading from their coat tails were carried to Dr Winter's small hospital where he was treating them as well as he could with what little he had. He figured that, with the right treatment, buttocks would heal, though sleeping on their backs might prove to be a problem.

No one knew what had happened to the captive Panchez; he had just melted into the night as had the gunman who had fired at Jude from behind the outhouse door.

'A good way to end a bad day,' Jude said to Josh. 'Only six of Nolan's men left alive and that includes us. And at least a dozen of Sullivan's men dead, either from gunshot wounds or by fire.'

'And Nolan's empire a heap of ashes too,' Jude reminded him needlessly. He turned to Sarah Jane. Despite being smeared with soot and ashes, she was, he could see, a mighty attractive young woman. 'What will you do now?' he asked her.

She was smiling ruefully behind her tears. 'I don't rightly know,' she said bravely. 'I have to thank you for saving my life. I thought I was going to die in there.'

'You have a deal of courage,' Jude assured her. 'And I think you'd have climbed out of that window on your own, though getting yourself down from that overhang might have given you a lot of trouble and broken a few bones.'

'I could have broken my neck if you hadn't been there to help me,' she told him. 'So I owe you my life, for what it's worth.'

He grinned, 'Your life is worth a whole lot more than dollars, and if you're offering it I'll be more than glad to accept it.'

Sarah Jane gazed at him in astonishment. 'You really mean

that?' she asked.

'I really mean it,' he affirmed.

'But you know what I've been through and the life I've had to live?'

Jude looked thoughtful for a moment. '*Had to live.*' He weighed the words in his mind. 'We all have to live according to what life throws at us. It's what we are inside that matters and I think you have a lot to offer inside, Miss Sarah Jane.'

'Then what about my colour?' she asked.

'What's colour got to do with it? When I look at you I see a dark skin with a golden glow coming from inside. That's what I see.'

'I think that fire has done roasted out your brains,' she said. 'Otherwise, I might take that as a compliment.'

'It might be a compliment and it might not be. It doesn't matter as long as it's true.'

Sarah Jane laughed. 'Where did you learn to talk like that?'

'I'm not sure I learned it at all,' he replied. 'It just sort of bubbles up occasionally. They tell me that's what the truth is about.'

'Then I think I'll take it is a compliment, Mr James.'

'I hope you will,' he said. 'In which case I guess you should come along with us.'

Sarah Jane's smile widened. 'Where are you going, Mr James?'

Jude looked at Josh and Josh made a wry face. 'Those are pretty speeches you just made, my friend, but we have to face the truth.' He gave Sarah Jane a sceptical grin. 'You know what we are, don't you?'

'Well,' Sarah Jane replied 'I know you're two very nice gentlemen. That's what I know.'

Josh gave that deep infectious laugh of his. 'I don't want to wear away my partner's confidence but the truth is we're just a couple of saddle bums without two beans to our name. So I can't say where we're going. But I do know one thing: that young woman back at the ranch and her pa will be expecting me to keep the promise I made to her.'

'What promise was that?' Sarah Jane asked.

Josh grinned. 'I promised to rescue that girl from slavery and that's what I mean to do.'

Now the town seemed to stir itself again. Men and women began to emerge from their houses. It was a modest-sized town and there were no more than a few hundred inhabitants and suddenly they were all milling around the burned-out buildings. No one seemed to know who was in charge. The sheriff lay dead. So everyone looked for a leader.

Then, surprisingly, the storekeeper Gullivant stepped forward. 'Well now,' he said. The cherubic smile had returned and he was still wearing his striped apron and, like everyone else, had his face smeared by soot from the fire. Yet he appeared to have acquired authority from somewhere. 'Well now,' he repeated, 'this has been a disaster, ladies and gentlemen, but we must look on the bright side, mustn't we? The whole town could have been burned down around us, but our noble neighbours have managed to save us and our properties are still intact . . . most of them, at least . . . so we must build on that, mustn't we?'

'Here, here,' someone shouted. 'Yes, we must,' someone else agreed.

'What about those people who died?' a woman asked.

'How did the fire start?' someone said.

No one knew the answer to that question. Most of the hotel staff who had survived lay groaning in the hospital.

'One of those gunmen upset a cooking stove,' a man said.

'How d'you know that?' someone asked.

Then Sarah Jane spoke up. 'It was one of Sullivan's men. He just threw a pan of hot fat over Mr Watmow, the manager. I saw it myself.'

'You saw it?'

'Yes, I saw it. And they shot Mr Watmow too. That's when it started. It happened so quickly nobody could do anything about it.'

'Well, folks, what's done is done,' the storekeeper said. 'But who's going to pay for all the damage, that's what I want to know?'

Everyone turned to Nolan who suddenly appeared to have diminished in size. He no longer had a cigar stuck in his mouth and he looked no more than an ordinary man. Yet he held up his hand for silence. Then he climbed on to the sidewalk to gain height.

'People of this fine town,' he said oratorically, 'this has been a long and painful night and we are all tired and many of us are grieving. . . .'

There was a loud murmur of agreement, though with an undertone of hostility.

'. . . But I make this promise to you good folk: this town will rise again. It will be rebuilt. Indeed, I will rebuild it myself. That hotel' – he swung round to point at the smouldering remains – 'that hotel will rise again. It will be grander than ever before and all those poor people who have perished will be—' He searched for the appropriate word.

Josh said, '*Vindicated.*'

Nolan beamed at him. That's the very word, Mr Appleseed, *vindicated.*' He seemed to roll the word in his mouth like a ripe plum. 'We will put up a cross on Main Street to remember them by for future generations.'

'But who's gonna pay for it?' someone shouted.

'And who's gonna pay for all the damage done?'

'And who will pay for all those poor townsfolk to be laid in the earth?'

There was mournful groan from the crowd.

Nolan held up his arm again and the people hushed down to listen. Nolan cleared his throat. 'I will pay for everything!' he shouted. 'I made this town grow and I will pay for it to grow yet again even it means spending my last dollar!'

There was a roar of approval from the crowd and one or two growls of disbelief.

'Can you believe that?' Josh said to Jude as they walked back through the town to pick up their horses.

'Can I believe that sugar candy grows on trees?' Jude replied. 'And do I believe the moon lives in the bottom of the lake?'

'What will happen now?' Sarah Jane asked Jude.

'We will ride back to the Nolan ranch and then take it from there,' Jude said.

Josh gave a sceptical grunt.

The townsfolk followed them through the town to the remuda where the wrangler Carlos was holding the horses. Now there were horses to spare since half of Nolan's men had died in the battle. Jude had wondered whether the remuda was safe from Sullivan's men but the horses were still all there.

'Can you ride, Sarah Jane?' Jude asked the girl.

'Didn't I tell you my pa was Indian?' she replied. 'You ever heard of an Indian who couldn't ride a horse?'

There were now seven people to be mounted and they had enough horses to spare. Sarah Jane looked over them and picked out the one she liked best. It was Jed Oliphant's mount and he sure wasn't going to need it any more because he would be riding to heaven or hell on swift invisible wings.

'So you're riding with us?' Nolan said to the girl, as though he had noticed her for the first time.

'Sarah Jane is my guest,' Jude said.

'Is that so?' Nolan looked at the girl critically.

'That's right, Mr Nolan.'

They mounted up and rode on down the trail towards the Nolan ranch. It was turning into quite a nice day, cool and refreshing after the suffocating storm. None of the riders had had any sleep, but somehow it didn't seem to matter. They rode on and held their heads high. The only one who looked somewhat mournful was Nolan himself. Maybe he was thinking about all he had lost in the conflagration and how he was going to carry out his promise to rebuild the town.

After half an hour he held up his arm like General Armstrong Custer and the party drew to a halt. 'Maybe it's time to take a break,' he said. 'I suggest we rest the horses and we can eat our hard tack.'

They dismounted and squatted by the creek where the horses could graze and drink. There wasn't much of what Nolan called hard tack, just a few biscuits and a little jerky they had in their saddle-bags. Josh stretched back and gazed at the sky. 'You know what, Mr James?'

'What is what, Mr Appleseed?' Jude replied.

'What is we've survived, Mr James, and that's a big what for a man who has not been killed, except for this shoulder of mine that does ache a little after all the trouble I've put it through.'

'Well, that's a big what,' Jude agreed. He held out his hand to Sarah Jane and she accepted it. Despite all the work she had been doing, she was had surprisingly soft hands.

The two other survivors were Jacko and Grillo, both of whom were half bloods. They spoke together, partly in Spanish and partly in English. Jacko rolled a quirly and passed it on to Grillo.

'You boys want a smoke?' he asked Jude and Josh.

'I don't think so,' Jude said. He didn't like to admit they made him sick.

Josh raised his hand and declined. 'Never got the habit,' he said.

Sarah Jane said, 'My daddy smoked bad stuff and that's what killed him. Ma warned him off it but it was too late. I might drink a drop or two now an' again, but I don't smoke.'

'Not even cigars?' Grillo asked her.

Nolan had managed to salvage one of his Havanas and was standing on the edge of the creek, puffing away thoughtfully.

That was when the first shot rang out. The bullet took Nolan's hat right off and spun it away across the water. The horses half spooked and lurched away from the creek. Nolan grabbed his Winchester and spun round, looking to see where the shot had come from.

The boys were up on their feet too, grabbing their weapons. Sarah Jane put her hand to her mouth to stifle a scream.

Josh pointed up at a rock formation just beyond the trees. 'It came from up there, Mr Nolan,' he shouted.

Nolan crouched down and put his hand to his eyes to shade out the sun. 'I believe you're right, boy,' he said.

Josh frowned: he didn't care for the term boy. It diminished him. But this was no time to argue.

Then came another shot, too close for comfort. One of the horses reared up and fell, and the rest of the horses started to whirl round and make for the woods.

'That was my horse!' Grillo cried out in alarm.

Then a laugh came from the rocks above. 'Well, Nolan, so you're still alive after all,' someone shouted. 'I guess you thought I was dead, but dead men rise again and I'm still here. It's me or you, Nolan. Which one of us will it be?'

Nolan held his Winchester high, searching for a target. 'Sullivan, I reckon it's gonna be me!' he shouted. His voice seemed to ricochet off the rocks and come back at him and on towards the flowing river.

The man in the rocks laughed again. 'You didn't have the *cojones* to meet me face to face in town, Nolan, and you haven't got the balls to face up to me now. You're just a puffed-up, rotting nobody, Nolan, and you should have burned in town or drowned in the storm, you know that?'

Nolan cupped his hands to his mouth to make a megaphone. 'You talk brave, Sullivan, while you're skulking behind the rocks up there. Why don't you come down and face up to me fair and square? I could bring you down before you had time to say "I'm here, Mister Nolan".'

Jude and Josh looked at each of them. 'This shouting match might go on all day,' Josh said. 'My guess is Sullivan is playing for time.'

'I think so too,' Jude agreed. 'He's just about as sly as a whole cage of monkeys.'

The answer came almost immediately and it came from the other side of the creek. Two horsemen dipped down into the creek and came riding fast but steadily across. The creek was neither wide nor deep and the riders had almost reached the other side before Nolan and the boys could stir themselves and they were firing their weapons as they came splashing across.

'So that's their game!' Josh said.

'And we've fallen right into their trap,' Jude agreed. 'Get down low,' he said to Sarah Jane. She didn't need to be told twice. She lay down flat behind a boulder and screened herself off from the river.

Jude seized his Winchester and took aim at one of the approaching riders. The two riders were so close now that

139

they were about to spur their mounts up the bank. Jude knew that if he fired on the nearest man, he ran the risk of bringing down Nolan himself. Nolan couldn't get his Winchester round to take aim, so he used it as a club. The rider bent over him and Nolan hit his leg hard. Then he reached up and dragged the man out of the saddle to the ground.

Josh fired a shot at the second man but he swerved off to his right and disappeared behind the rearing horses. Grillo and Jacko ran towards the animals, firing wildly, and the mounts plunged into the creek and made for the opposite bank.

Nolan was still hitting the first rider with his Winchester and the man jerked back and fell into the creek where he attempted to swim, but he didn't get far. Nolan turned his Winchester, levered it, and fired a shot. The man twitched and disappeared below the water. Nolan then ran along the bank and fired a shot at the other rider who threw up his arms, fell from his prancing horse, and also disappeared into the creek.

Nolan peered up at the rocks, but there was no movement and no more shots. 'Well, we brought down two,' he crowed. 'Now we just have Sullivan to deal with.' He looked excited, even triumphant.

'Maybe Sullivan pulled out to save his skin,' Josh speculated.

'I don't think so,' Nolan said. 'Sullivan has a mind like a savage. He won't stop until he wins or dies.'

'So what do we do now?' Jude asked.

'What we do is we climb up there and smoke him out. That's what we do,' Nolan said. Jude had never seen him so angry and steamed up before.

Josh looked up at the rocks and considered tactics. 'That isn't gonna be easy, Mr Nolan. We don't know how many there are up there, do we?'

'If we can get under cover of those rocks, Sullivan can't get a bead on us,' Nolan said. 'So what we do is fan out and climb up there by separate routes. I'm going up there and I want you, Josh, and you, Jude, to come with me.'

'What about us, boss?' Grillo asked.

'You wait down here and look after the horses,' Nolan told him.

'The horses have stampeded to the other side of the creek,' Jacko said.

'Well, ride on after them and round them up!' Nolan shouted in exasperation.

Grillo and Jacko ran down to the creek side and peered across. The two corpses were floating away downstream. Nolan, Josh and Jude started towards the rocks. But they didn't get far. Jude looked up and saw a rider silhouetted against the sky. The rider turned and took a wild shot at them and shouted, 'I'll see you in hell, Nolan, I'll see you in hell.'

'Don't waste your energy climbing up there, Mr Nolan,' Josh said. 'My guess is hell's a lot closer to the creek.'

Nolan was almost grinding his teeth in his fury. 'I think you're right, boy,' he agreed. 'Better to round up the horses.'

They went down to the edge of the creek. Grillo and Jacko and the wrangler Carlos were calling in the horses who seemed to have settled down to graze again.

'Have they gone?' the girl asked.

'Sullivan's pulled out,' Jude explained.

'It doesn't mean he's gone,' Josh said. 'It means he's changed tactics. Best if we stick by the creek until the mounts are rounded up.'

The wrangler was good with horses and they seemed to respond to his call, and, after a short time, he and Grillo and Jacko brought the horses splashing across the creek again.

Then the group veered away from the creek and made for

141

the trail that led in the direction of the Nolan ranch.

'Keep yourselves steady and alert,' Nolan said. He stuck another cigar in his mouth and mounted up. Then he rode on like Caesar making towards Rome.

'That guy's as crazy as hell,' Josh said to Jude.

'He and Sullivan both,' Jude agreed. 'We've got two crazy men in opposition here.'

Sarah Jane was riding close beside Jude and he put his hand on her arm. 'Keep close and don't worry,' he said. 'We'll get out of this together.'

She gave him an encouraging smile.

They rode on along the trail which was quite well marked. The creek was now way off to their right. They had ridden on for no more than half a mile when the trail narrowed and continued between a heavily wooded area closer to the creek. Jude thought, If Sullivan knows the trail well, this a likely place for another bushwhacking. And he was right. A rider appeared from the trees and stood on the trail ahead of them. It was Dean Sullivan.

Nolan raised his arm and they stopped. Sullivan was no more than a hundred feet ahead. Jude could see from his expression that he was chuckling to himself as though he had already won a great tactical victory.

'What do you want, Sullivan?' Nolan shouted. 'Haven't you had enough yet?'

'Well now, Nolan, what I want is your hide, that's what I want,' Sullivan shouted back.

Nolan shifted in the saddle. 'That's a big want, Sullivan. One of my boys could shoot you right out of the saddle, you know that?'

'Well, that's an interesting thought,' Sullivan said, 'but I don't think that's the way it's gonna be. I have another theory entirely.'

'And what's that?'

Sullivan held his head on one side. 'My theory is you're gonna get right off your horse and face me like a man.'

'So that's what you think?' Nolan turned and gave Jude a quizzical smile. 'You hear what the man says?'

'I hear well enough,' Jude replied.

'You want me to take a pop at him, Mr Nolan?' Jacko asked.

Nolan grinned. 'Thank you, Jacko, but I can fight my own corner.' He nodded towards Sullivan again. 'OK, Sullivan, this is it. No Winchesters, just six shooters, me and you.'

Sullivan nodded. 'What we do is we dismount and walk towards one another to the count of six. That's if you have the balls?'

'One shot each,' Nolan said. 'And who's gonna count?'

There was a pause. Way off they could hear the rush of water from the creek and the tree tops quivering momentarily, either with grief or from the foolhardiness of mankind.

Then Josh spoke up. 'If this nonsense must continue I'll be the judge. I'll ride out halfway between you. Then, on my signal, you walk forward six paces and shoot. One shot each and if no one scores a hit we part in peace. Is that fair enough?'

There was another pause, long enough to hear a bird singing high up in the trees.

'Very well,' Sullivan said, 'one shot each but who's gonna check the shooters?'

'I'll check the shooters,' Jude volunteered. 'If you place your guns on the trail, I'll check each one and take them to the other man to make sure nobody cheats. Is that agreeable, gentlemen?'

'That's agreeable,' Nolan said. He drew his Colt and handed it to Jude. Jude emptied the chambers until there was one bullet left. He then took the Colt and walked across to Sullivan.

Sullivan took his Colt from its holster and held it out. Jude checked it and handed it back. He stood for a moment looking Sullivan in the eye. Sullivan was almost as tall as him. He had reddish straggly hair and freckles on his face. He looked almost boyish except for the vicious gleam in his eye. 'You sure you want to go through with this, Mr Sullivan?' Jude asked.

Sullivan grinned. 'I can't wait to blow Nolan off the face of the earth,' he declared and Jude saw his eye twitch.

Jude handed him back his Colt. 'You're a damned fool, Sullivan, you know that?'

'We're all fools,' Sullivan replied. 'The whole world's a nest of fools.'

Jude walked back to Nolan and saw that Nolan was looking somewhat uncomfortable. 'You don't have to do this, Mr Nolan,' he said. 'Sullivan's a desperate man. If we just ride on there isn't much he can do. He'll have to get off the trail and let us pass.'

Nolan looked him squarely in the eye. 'We'd have to trample him down first,' he said. 'This is a matter of honour, Mr James. Don't you understand that? Out here a man lives or dies according to his code. A man without honour might just as well be dead as a dog, anyway.'

Jude scrutinized him and saw he was unyielding. 'Well, if that's the way you want it, Mr Nolan, that's the way it has to be.'

Nolan took his Colt, checked the chambers, and thrust it into its holster.

Jude held up his hand. 'We're all set,' he said to Josh.

Josh stepped to one side. 'OK,' he said. 'I'm going to count to six. When I get to six, you walk forward six paces and draw your guns and fire. Those are the rules. You understand?'

The two duellists nodded their assent.

144

Jude motioned to the rest of Nolan's party to clear the trail so that nobody would be hit by a stray bullet, and they drew their horses to one side. But then the girl Sarah Jane cried out in a loud lamenting tone, 'Isn't anybody going to put a stop to this madness? Haven't we seen enough bloodshed? In the name of God stop this before it's too late!'

But it was already too late. Josh was about to start the countdown.

'Get back!' Jude shouted, and Sarah Jane's horse skittered to the right as though it understood what was about to happen.

The two men stared at one another and then tensed themselves to walk into eternity. And Josh started the count. One to six is a short count, yet it seemed to Jude to go on forever. The two men walked until they were no more than fifteen feet apart from one another. There was no lightning draw. It seemed to happen in slow motion. Jude saw them reach down simultaneously and draw their weapons. Both aimed from the hip and the explosions came as one.

As they fired a huge flock roosting in the trees took off in panic and flew away screeching a warning to the world in general.

Then, as though the fist of the devil had appeared between them, both men were thrust back. Nolan staggered three paces and dropped down; Sullivan lurched and fell down on one knee and dropped his gun. He swayed for a moment and then reached down into his boot and came up with a small derringer in his shaking hand.

Josh stepped towards him and shouted, 'Just one shot! That's the rule!'

Sullivan turned slowly and tried to raise the derringer but it was too heavy for his dying fingers and it dropped harmlessly on to the trail. An expression of bewilderment appeared in his eyes and he keeled forward and his head hit the trail with a dull thud.

Nolan pulled himself up and struggled to rise to his feet. He looked down at his bloody chest in amazement. 'I've been hit, Mr James,' he gasped. It was the last thing he ever said. He stared for a moment at the body of his enemy, coughed up a deal of blood, and dropped down dead.

CHAPTER ELEVEN

Josh looked down at the dead faces and took off his hat. 'Well, I'll be damned,' he muttered. 'Who'd have believed it?' He held his hat to his chest and bowed his head. 'Doesn't that seem an awful waste of life, Mr James?'

'They did what they wanted to, Mr Appleseed,' Jude said. 'It's what some people call Fate.'

'Well, that guy Fate has a lot to answer for,' Josh announced gloomily. 'I don't think I want any more to do with him.' Jude saw his hand quivering as he held the hat to his chest.

Now the other men came forward. Jacko and Grillo and Carlos the wrangler doffed their Stetsons and Grillo started muttering low in Spanish. It was as though he had suddenly been transmogrified into a priest. The wrangler also had his hat in his hand and he looked at the other two as though for guidance.

Sarah Jane stared hard at the two bodies but she didn't cry out. She just choked back her tears and looked indignant. Then she turned to Jude. 'This shouldn't have happened,' she said quietly. 'You shouldn't have let it happen.'

'There's nothing we could have done to stop it, Miss Sarah Jane,' Josh piped up. 'Like Jude said, it was a matter of Fate.'

'Well, Fate is a wicked critter,' the girl said, 'That's what I think.'

There was a moment of silence. Jude could still hear that persistent bird singing out triumphantly from the top of the tree but the sound of the flowing river was strangely muted.

'What do we do now?' Grillo asked.

'Well we can't leave them here for the coyotes and the buzzards to feed on,' Jacko said. 'We need to show some respect for the dead, *quien sabe*?'

Grillo crossed himself. '*Sí, señor.*'

Then, as if on cue, they heard the sound of horses approaching along the trail towards the town and the stagecoach appeared round a bend. The driver drew the horses to a halt and he and the man riding shotgun climbed down to investigate. 'What's happened here?' the driver asked.

'There's been a shooting,' Josh said. 'That's what's happened.'

'Two men killed,' shotgun said, looking down at the dead men, 'and unless I'm mistaken that's Mr Nolan himself.'

'Nolan and Sullivan,' Grillo told him.

'Did you see it happen?' the driver asked.

'It was a shoot out,' Jacko explained. 'We saw the whole thing. Could have been killed ourselves.'

'What do you aim to do now?' the driver asked.

Jude and Josh exchanged glances. It seemed that, if there were decisions be made, they would have to make them. Now several additional faces were staring out of the windows of the stagecoach and two people had disembarked to examine the bodies.

'Well, now,' Jude said, 'why don't you ride on into town and tell the funeral director there's a dead man called Dean Sullivan waiting to be taken in for decent burial, and on your way you might see two bodies floating in the creek, not to mention one dead horse.'

'Is that so?' said the driver. 'Two men and one horse.'

'That is definitely so,' Jude replied sombrely, 'and when you get to town you might also notice The Grand Hotel has been burned down to the ground along with several other buildings.'

'And the sheriff's been killed too,' Grillo added, 'together with a lot of other *hombres.*'

The stagecoach driver exchanged glances with shotgun. 'Are you kidding me?' he asked in amazement.

'That's the truth, *señor,*' Jacko said.

The driver opened his mouth wide in astonishment. 'There must have been quite a shindig in town.'

'You can quote me on that,' Jude said.

One of the passengers looked down at Nolan's body, and said, 'What do you aim to do with Mr Nolan here?'

Jude and Josh exchanged glances again.

'Since Mr Nolan can't speak up for himself,' Jude said, 'we have to speak for him and I figure he'll want to be buried on the ranch so he can look out over his property with pride.'

The driver looked perplexed. 'So you figure that's what he would want?'

'Maybe that's his Fate,' Josh said.

The driver shrugged. 'Well, if that's what you want.'

'And don't expect a bright welcome in town,' Josh said. 'They've been through a very bad time there. If there's such a place as hell that was it.'

'We'll bear that in mind.' The passengers got into the coach and the driver and shotgun climbed on to their seats. The driver whipped up the horses and the stagecoach rumbled on.

'Not the best of homecomings,' Jude said, as they hoisted Nolan's body on to the back of his horse. The horse glanced sideways at them but didn't seem unduly concerned.

As they rode on, Grillo and Jacko exchanged opinions in

149

Spanish which neither Jude nor Josh could understand. Jude could only guess what they were saying from the tone of their voices.

'Do you savvy Spanish?' Jude asked Sarah Jane who was riding beside him.

'They speak about the future,' she said. 'They don't know what will happen now the boss has passed on.'

Jude nodded. He was thinking about the future too. He and Josh had seen enough bloodshed to last a lifetime, maybe two lifetimes. It might be best for them to ride on away from this unholy mess and look for something a little more congenial. But then he looked at Sarah Jane and thought, I seem to have an obligation to this young woman. She deserves a whole lot better than this heap of shit.

When they rode up to the ranch, Jake and his daughter Nancy came out to meet them. Jake stared at Nolan's body in astonishment. 'What in hell's happened to Mr Nolan? Can this be the the the truth?' he declared.

'Well, it's no fiction,' Jude said. 'He got himself killed.' Then he told them about the shoot out with Sullivan.

'So Sullivan's dead too!' the old man marvelled.

'Sullivan and a heap of other men,' Jude said. 'Women as well.'

'The town's in bad shape,' Josh told them. He was looking at Nancy and she and Sarah Jane exchanged glances. 'Is that you, Sarah Jane?' Nancy asked. 'You're looking quite out of yourself.'

'We've been through a difficult time,' Sarah Jane said. Jude nodded in agreement. He liked the way Sarah Jane spoke, without undue exaggeration and without focusing on her own particular plight.

'What do we do now?' the old man enquired.

Everyone looked at Jude. 'What we do is we lift Mr Nolan gently down from his horse and carry him into the barn and lay him down. Then we dig a grave in a good position where he can lie and look out over his property and meditate on the future.'

'The future's an awful long stretch of time,' Jake said.

'Time's so long it stretches right into eternity,' Josh agreed. 'But I guess he won't worry too much about that.'

They carried his body into the barn and laid it on a bed of straw. Jude thought, how strange, he looks almost as though he knows the secret of the universe and isn't about to disclose it.

'All he needs is one of those fat cigars in his mouth,' Jacko suggested.

'I don't think they smoke where he's gone,' Grillo said.

Then Nancy spoke up. 'Someone should tell Mrs Nolan.'

'Mrs Nolan?' Josh said. 'Who is Mrs Nolan?'

Jake rolled his eyes. 'You might not have seen her but she's here. She lives in that cabin up there.' He pointed up the hill where a small log cabin stood with smoke rising from the chimney.

'You mean Nolan was married?' Jude asked.

Jake nodded and held his head on one side. 'Been married time out of mind,' he said. 'You don't see her but she's there. And I should warn you, she's kind of delicate.' He rolled his eyes to the sky to suggest some sort of nervous condition.

'You mean she's crazy?' Josh asked.

'Mrs Nolan isn't crazy,' Nancy said. 'She's just sensitive in the head.'

'Then what do you suggest we should do?' Jude asked.

'I'll walk up myself,' Nancy declared, 'and maybe Sarah Jane will come with me?'

Jude and Josh and the boys busied themselves with the horses and presently Sarah Jane returned.

'Mrs Nolan is coming down with Nancy right away,' she said.

They looked towards the cabin and saw the two figures emerge. Jude expected to see a somewhat haggard woman, like a deformed witch, but the woman he saw surprised him. Mrs Nolan was around forty, and she looked . . . well, elegant. As she drew close she checked the men over with mournful eyes.

'So they tell me my husband has been killed,' she said, a slight tremor in her voice.

'We've laid him in the barn, ma'am,' Jude told her. 'That's if you want to see him.'

'No, no,' she said. 'I couldn't bear that. I prefer to think of him alive.' She stepped up to Jude. 'And who are you, sir?'

Jude smiled faintly. 'I'm Jude James, ma'am. I was with Mr Nolan when he died.'

'Well, that's a blessing.' She held out a delicate hand and Jude took it. Her fingers were like the fragile petals of a rare flower. Then she turned to Josh. 'And who is this?' she asked somewhat regally.

Josh gave a slight nod of the head. 'I'm Josh Appleseed,' he said proudly.

Mrs Nolan smiled. 'Appleseed.' She rolled the word on her tongue like she was from one of the Southern states. 'That's a nice sounding name. Were you once a slave, Mr Appleseed?'

Josh gave her one of his broad smiles. 'Indeed, I was, Mrs Nolan, but now I'm glad to say I'm a free man.'

She smiled again. 'I'm from the South, Mr Appleseed, and my daddy was a plantation owner, and I'm glad you are free.'

'Thank you, ma'am. I'm sort of glad myself.'

A slight shadow passed over the lady's face. 'Were you with my husband when he died, Mr Appleseed?'

'Yes, ma'am, I saw him die,' Josh said.

'I see what they mean when they said she was delicate,' Jude said to Josh later.

Josh smiled. 'I agree. Delicate isn't exactly the right word, Mr James. I think out of time and place would be a better description.'

'And what do you mean by that, Mr Appleseed?'

Josh shrugged. 'Mrs Nolan comes from a slave-owning family. Somewhere, sometime, she met Nolan and they got married. But they were an ill-assorted pair and it didn't work out. That's why she lives in that cabin up there, waiting for eternity, and now eternity has come right up to her door and knocked on it with a clenched fist.'

Jude nodded. 'Well, whoever eternity is, now that Nolan is fluttering up there beyond the clouds, do you think he told Mrs Nolan who owns the spread?' he asked.

'I don't know about that, Mr James, but I think one of us has to find out.'

'How do we do that, Mr Appleseed?'

'Well now, Mr James, either you or me needs to ride into town and investigate. Mr Nolan must have had a lawyer somewhere and that lawyer probably holds Mr Nolan's last will and testament. In my opinion you should ride in tomorrow morning and sort the whole thing out.'

'Well, I agree on the procedure, Mr Appleseed, but why don't you go?'

'That's because you're sort of the colour of a brick building and that lawyer is probably the colour of a brick building too, so you will likely carry more weight.'

Josh and Jude slept that night like angels somewhere between earth and heaven, and next morning Jude saddled his horse early and rode back along the trail towards town. He passed the spot where they had laid Sullivan's body but was pleased to see that it had gone. Well, someone respects the dead around here, he thought.

When he got to town, he dismounted outside the store and walked in. The stout storekeeper appeared almost immediately. 'Good morning to you,' he said. 'I hear Mr Nolan is dead and they brought in Mr Sullivan's body a little earlier this morning. What can I do for you, Mr James?'

'You can point me in the direction of the lawyer's office, Mr Gullivant.'

Gullivant stepped out on to the sidewalk and pointed in the direction of the burned-out hotel. 'You ride down there a piece and you'll see a sign, J.P. Sanderson. He's the lawyer and I guess he knows about Mr Nolan's affairs.' His wide brow creased over. 'This is a terrible thing, Mr James. Mr Nolan owned most of this town. So I don't know what will happen now.'

'Well, Mr Gullivant,' Jude said, 'I don't figure you need to worry too much on that score. Like Mr Nolan said, this town will rise from its ashes like the famous phoenix.'

'What's the phoenix, some kind of saint?' the storekeeper asked.

'I believe it was a bird, Mr Gullivant. I'll tell you about it later.' Jude tipped his Stetson and rode on.

When he reached the heap of ashes and debris that had once been The Grand Hotel he saw the Reverend Jeremy Justice and Doc Winter standing together watching men searching through the rubble.

'So you're not dead,' the Reverend Jerry said to Jude.

'No, it seems I'm still in the land of the living,' Jude replied. 'Anything you've heard to the contrary is a wild exaggeration.'

Doc Winter gave him a sceptical grin. 'And how about that friend of yours, Mr Appleseed?'

'Mr Appleseed is also in the land of the living, thanks to you, Doctor. So, are they still finding bodies in there?'

'The whole thing's been a tragedy,' the Reverend Jerry said. 'I think it's eleven bodies at the last count.'

'What happens to the town now?' the doc asked.

'That's what I'm here to find out.' Jude smiled and rode on to the sign with the legend J.P. Sanderson, Attorney at Law. He dismounted and tied his horse to the hitching rail. He walked across the sidewalk and knocked on the door.

'Come in!' a voice called in response.

When Jude opened the door, he saw a lean, lantern-jawed individual sitting behind a desk that seemed about a mile wide. 'Who are you?' the man demanded.

'I'm Jude James, sir, and I've come to report a death.'

J.P. Sanderson rapped on his desk. 'Cut the cackle, Mr James. We've had at least twenty deaths in the last twenty-four hours.'

Jude took off his hat and sat down on a chair opposite the lawyer. 'I'm talking about the death of Mr Nolan,' he said, 'in a shooting between him and Mr Sullivan a few miles out of town.'

'Ah!' J.P. Sanderson suddenly leaned forward and became a little more amiable. 'Have you come on Mrs Nolan's behalf?'

'Not exactly,' Jude said. 'I've come to inform you so that you can ride out to the ranch some time and read out the will. As you may know, Mrs Nolan is a somewhat delicate lady, so I rode into town to report the matter on her behalf.'

Sanderson nodded and relaxed a little more. When his lantern jaw broke into a grin he looked somewhat less like the living dead and more like a human being with blood in his veins. He even spoke more like a human being.

'This has been a terrible business,' he said, 'this feud between Nolan and Sullivan. It goes right back to the war. I believe they were in the same regiment, but war does terrible things to a man. Sullivan thought Nolan had let down the regiment, so he wanted revenge and that twisted his nature and he became a demon.' He sat back and meditated for a moment. 'And now they're both dead. Would you care for some refreshment, Mr James? A mug of coffee, perhaps?'

'Thank you, Mr Sanderson. That would be most welcome.'

Jude rode back from town feeling he had accomplished his mission. And he wasn't alone. As he rode out towards the ranch he met the Reverend Jerry Justice on his big black horse.

'That's a fine black horse you've got there,' Jude said.

'She's a beauty, isn't she?' the preacher replied. 'D'you mind if I ride out to the ranch with you? I need to make arrangements for the good man's funeral and bring some comfort to Nolan's widow.'

Jude turned in the saddle. 'Why do you call Nolan a good man?' he said. 'Nolan was no better and no worse than the rest of us.'

The Reverend Jerry raised his eyebrows. 'I believe you're right, Mr James,' he said. 'And does that apply to Dean Sullivan too?'

Jude looked down at his horse's mane and considered matters. 'I didn't know Dean Sullivan, sir. All I ever saw of him was at the end of the barrel of a gun, and that kind of prejudices a man somewhat.'

The Reverend Jerry gave him a quizzical look. 'I do believe you're a man of faith, Mr James. Have you considered that?'

Jude gave him a startled look like a bird that sees a man close to for the first time. 'I haven't given the matter a lot of thought,' he replied.

'Well, maybe you should,' the Reverend Jerry said with a cryptic smile.

*

They buried Nolan on a hill overlooking the spread. Jude, Josh and the boys dug a deep grave in the ground and the funeral director brought a simple casket from town. The Reverend Jerry said a few appropriate prayers over the casket and it was lowered into the grave. He threw a small bunch of wild flowers on to the casket on behalf of Mrs Nolan who was too delicate to attend.

Jacko then stepped forward and raised his Colt revolver. 'I think we should honour Mr Nolan with a round or two,' he said solemnly.

'I agree,' Grillo added. He drew his own gun and they discharged their weapons into the air like soldiers firing a loud farewell.

Then Jacko and Grillo exchanged satisfied glances.

Back in the eating-hall Jake and his daughter with a little help from Sarah Jane, produced quite a presentable meal. The tables were all pushed together to form one long table and they sat on either side in no particular order except that at one end places were reserved for J.P. Sanderson and his wife Noreen, and one empty space reserved for Mrs Nolan herself. At the last moment she appeared wearing a long dark dress. Everyone rose to their feet as if to greet a duchess or a queen, and the Reverend Jerry said a heartfelt prayer that seemed to go on for ever. Present at table, as well as Jude, Josh, Jacko and Grillo and the other ranch hands, were Doc Winter and his wife, and a number of other worthies from the town. There was, in fact, quite a festive air to the occasion.

At the end of the feast the Reverend Jerry stood up and rapped on the table for silence. 'Now, ladies and gentlemen!' he said in a good strong voice. 'Don't you worry, I'm not about to make a speech, but I want you to listen carefully because Mr Sanderson intends to read out the late Mr Nolan's last will and testament.'

There was a murmur of interest as Sanderson rose majestically and put on a pair of small spectacles that made him look somewhat like an owl with its face feathers plucked out. He spoke in a laborious tone as though it was all in the line of business.

There were no surprises in the will, except the amount of assets involved which, if not enormous, were considerable. Nolan had left everything to his wife Lucinda '*under the wise guidance of Mr J.P. Sanderson*'.

At that point the lawyer paused and Mrs Nolan burst into tears. It was the first time she had shown any emotion since her husband's death.

'What happens now?' Jude asked Josh after the proceedings.

'Life carries on as usual,' Josh said.

Josh looked doubtful. 'Life never carries on as usual, Mr James,' he said. 'There are always changes. That's what life is about. If we don't change life, it changes us. So what do we do now, I ask?'

They didn't have long to wait. A couple of days later Nancy appeared at their table. 'Mrs Nolan is coming down from her cabin with Mr Sanderson,' she announced. 'She has some important things to say.'

Josh looked at Jude and Jude shrugged his shoulders. 'I think the big change is about to be announced,' he said. 'So get yourself ready to move on, Mr Appleseed.'

All eyes turned to the door as J.P. Sanderson and Mrs Nolan appeared. For a moment no one spoke. Everyone expected the lawyer to make the announcement, but they were in for a big surprise. Mrs Nolan came to the table and stared at everyone in turn. And when she spoke there was no delicacy in her voice. It was as though her old plantation days had returned.

'Well, now, you all,' she began, 'I want you to listen up and take in what I have to say.' She paused and swallowed hard. 'Now my dear husband has passed on and left me in charge, I want to make one thing clear: the law of the gun is over and we want peace.'

She paused again but there was no response. Everyone was staring at her in amazement. Who was this strange woman who had emerged from the cabin on the hill?

Then she gave a small cough and went on. 'I want you to know something,' she said. 'From now on I won't tolerate guns on this property except when it comes to hunting or defence. If you agree to that, you can all stay. If not, you can collect your wages and move on. I will pay your wages in full, and that is your choice.'

There was another pause. Nobody knew quite how to respond. Then Jude gave a clap and everyone joined in and Jacko piped up with a cheer.

Lucinda Nolan held up her hand and smiled. 'I mean to build up this ranch and make a good honest business of it and Mr Sanderson has agreed to help me in that.' She glanced towards Jude and Josh along the table. 'And in future, Mr James and Mr Appleseed will be my top hands, if they agree.'

Jude glanced at Josh and saw a reddish glow illuminate his face.

'Thank you, ma'am,' Jude said. 'We agree to that.'

'Yes, we sure do,' Josh beamed.

Later in their small cabin which was no bigger than a store cupboard, Jude and Josh sat talking.

'You know what, Mr Appleseed,' Jude said.

'What's that, Mr James?'

'I've come to a decision.'

'A decision!' Josh wagged his head and grinned. 'You

159

amaze me, Mr James. But I can guess what it is.'

'You can, Mr Appleseed?'

'My guess is you aim to ask that young woman Miss Sarah Jane to marry you.'

'Well, I'll be blessed!' Jude said. 'You sure guessed that one right!'

Josh said, 'That's because I had the very same thought myself, except that, in my case, it was Miss Nancy I had in mind.'

The two young ladies concerned put up modest resistance, but their defences fell down as quickly as the walls of Jericho. The two parties had a joint ceremony in the little chapel that the Reverend Jerry had established in town and then a reception back at the Nolan ranch. There were, of course, speeches and jokes, some of them quite rude, but everything went well. Mrs Nolan had apportioned two sizeable plots where they could build their respective cabins.

Lucinda Nolan turned out to be a lot more than a shrinking violet. She had a good head for business and a determination to build up the ranch where she would rear cattle, horses, and even hens and pigs.

As for the town, she conferred with J.P.Sanderson and together they established a plan. The Grand Hotel rose again like the phoenix from its ashes and became even grander. And Lucinda decreed that a small monument should be built in the town square as a tribute to all who had died in that short but bitter struggle between her husband and the Sullivan gang.

The monument still stands in the town square and the town was renamed Nolan's Place.